A WATERY GR

Bodie emptied
slugs had no v

The launch
their plight. Now,
dead in the water, the engi
and Doyle heard the launch's engi

The white bow wave creamed higher. The launch turned from a long, low silhouette into just a sharp prow and two curling waves, one each side.

Doyle yelled, 'He's going to ram us!'

The launch raced on, spraying water, leaping at them like a torpedo.

Also by Ken Blake in Sphere Books:

THE PROFESSIONALS 1: WHERE THE JUNGLE ENDS
THE PROFESSIONALS 2: LONG SHOT
THE PROFESSIONALS 3: STAKE OUT
THE PROFESSIONALS 4: HUNTER HUNTED
THE PROFESSIONALS 5: BLIND RUN
THE PROFESSIONALS 6: FALL GIRL
THE PROFESSIONALS 7: HIDING TO NOTHING
THE PROFESSIONALS 8: DEAD RECKONING
THE PROFESSIONALS 9: NO STONE
THE PROFESSIONALS 10: CRY WOLF
THE PROFESSIONALS 12: FOX HOLE
THE PROFESSIONALS 13: THE UNTOUCHABLES

THE PROFESSIONALS:
Spy Probe

KEN BLAKE

Based on the original screenplays by
Tony Barwick and Christopher Wicking

SPHERE BOOKS LIMITED
30-32 Gray's Inn Road, London WC1X 8JL

First published by Sphere Books Ltd 1981

Reprinted 1981, 1982

TRADE
MARK

Set in Photon Baskerville

Printed and bound in Great Britain by
Collins, Glasgow

Chapter One

The paving stones slapped up hard through the soles of Ray Doyle's trainers as he pelted along the street. He'd been running for half a mile. His face looked frowzy from two days' growth of beard, and the old navy-blue donkey jacket he wore shone with wear. His face with the beard looked unkempt with his tangle of curls all blowing as he ran. That face of Doyle's also looked remarkably hard and grim and dark with purpose.

The red-painted telephone box on the corner had a lean to it, it lay over one-sided as though trying to gain protection from the grey grimy walls against the local vandals.

The street looked grubby, with blank walls and rows of tattered placards peeling from hoardings, with windows broken and planked over. Dust and papers blew in the gutter.

Doyle wrenched the phone box door open. Most of the glass had vanished from the small window-squares, and if there was anything left of the phone books it looked as though it had been through a paper-shredder. He hung on to the door for a moment, taking two deep breaths. He was not so much panting as feeling the indignity of this pantomime.

He started to search the phone box.

Across the street the ends of two abandoned warehouses were connected – or partially connected – by a rotting wooden fence. The planks were gradually disappearing as the meths fraternity took away their firewood for chilly nights.

Hidden in the rear of the fence and peering out through a gap, Ferris watched the phone box. He was a strongly-built man in his mid thirties; but he was running to fat. As he kept a keen eye on Doyle he took a chocolate bar from his pocket and began to strip the paper and foil away. He shook his head as Doyle searched round, the blue donkey jacket clearly visible.

Presently Doyle came out of the phone box, kicked an empty beer can aside, and stared up and down the deserted street. His face looked real mean. He started to walk away, hunching his shoulders into the donkey jacket, and the phone rang.

Doyle stared at the phone box for a moment. Then he went back ana took the phone off the hook.

'Hello.'

The voice on the other end of the line held a slight but distinctive mid-European accent. Doyle thought of it as the Brown Bear voice.

Brown Bear said: 'I'm pleased to hear you are still with us.'

More than a hint of truculence suffused Doyle's answer.

'You said I'd *find* a message.'

The little point was completely ignored by the phone voice.

'Here is your next point of contact.'

Doyle drew a breath.

'Look, you've run me half way across London. I want to know what's going on.'

The Brown Bear voice seemed to become more distant.

'If you do not wish to proceed, that is your prerogative.'

Doyle put his lips together and the muscles in his cheeks jumped. Finally he said: 'All right.'

'River Street. Do you know it?'

'Yeah. I know it.'

Brown Bear said: 'In five minutes.'

A flush of indignant anger instinctively spreading in Doyle had to be quenched; he had to play this in a tough way, but, equally, he had to be prepared to go along with the preparations. So, in a hard voice, he snapped out: 'Five minutes . . . It's nearly a mile . . .'

The phone went dead.

The mysterious caller had disconnected in mid-sentence.

Doyle took the handset from his ear, stared at it as though it had magically changed into a snake, and then slammed it back on the rest. He shoved the phone box door open with his shoulder. He stomped out onto the hard pavement and then, philosophically, started to run towards River Street.

The paving stones were *damned* hard on the soles of his feet.

Across the way, lurking behind his broken-down fence, Ferris smiled fatly around the chunk of chocolate distending his cheek. He wadded up the paper and foil and flipped it away. He looked fat with satisfaction.

'One,' he said to himself, very smugly. 'One born every day of the week.'

When Doyle had panted off out of sight, Ferris stretched and ducked through the gap in the fence. He strolled with all the time in the world to his car parked a way up the road. He'd kept an eye on it besides watching the phone box. This neighbourhood might be decrepit and look deserted, but they'd have the wheels off and the fittings off in an instant if you let them. He got in and started up and tooled the car gently along, following the direction Doyle had taken to River Street.

He cut through Dock Way and angled up Albemarle Street and so tooled the car gently into the end of River Street. The phone box was about half way down, lonely and vandalised against a brick wall past the end of a shed whose windows were boarded up. Ferris brought the car to a halt on the opposite side of the road from the phone box.

Then he lounged back in the driving seat.

He checked his wristwatch.

Right on time, when the minute hand reached the luminous figure, the telephone began to ring. Five minutes on the dot.

Ferris lounged, looking along the street. He was smiling, enjoying the situation.

Ray Doyle slapped those abused feet of his down on the concrete, pounding along. He reached the box with the sound of the phone shrilling imperatively. He yanked tne door open and practically fell inside.

The receiver came off in a scooped motion. He drew three huge lungfulls of air, getting his breath. He felt mad clean through.

The Brown Bear voice said: 'You're twenty seconds late.'

'Yeah,' said Doyle. He drew another shaky breath. 'Yeah, well, that's it. I've had enough.'

The voice on the phone said: 'I'm inclined to agree. Go to the car across the street.'

The line clicked and sounded like a bottomless well.

Doyle put the phone back very gently.

He looked through the dusty windows at the car on the other side of the road.

Just a car. An unremarkable, black Cortina. He shoved the phone box door open.

From the open window of the car Ferris waved a casual arm.

There was no traffic about. Doyle walked across and stood by the driver's window. He stood warily, poised, half bending down.

The driver looked up, a fattish man in a dark jacket. A brown smear at the corner of his mouth took Doyle's attention.

Ferris said: 'Ever thought about the Olympics? You'd do well in the ten thousand metres.'

Doyle just glared.

'Get in, the man wants to meet you.'

'What man?'

'Don't ask silly questions. Get in.'

As this was the point of the whole operation, Doyle walked around the car and got in. He sat back. Sitting down came as a luxury. Ferris started up and the Cortina moved off, its tyres crunching over an abandoned cardboard box.

Ferris kept his gaze on the road but from time to time he glanced sideways at Doyle. That sort of behaviour in a driver always gave Doyle the jitters, and Bodie, too.

'So,' began Ferris. 'You're ready to go anywhere and do anything, are you?'

This was the play Doyle had made, and now he had passed the first ridiculous but tiring test, he was anxious to get on with it.

'If the money's right.'

'No problem there, my son.' Ferris turned out of River Street, and presently the traffic began to thicken. 'Just how far would you go?'

'What d'you mean?'

'Would you break a few heads?'

Doyle put on a mean tone. 'Try me.'

Ferris nodded to himself. 'Would you kill?'

The surprise Doyle exhibited was only partly a sham. The nub of the exercise had been quickly reached. 'What?'

'I said, would you kill?'

'Kill?' Now Doyle put on the bewildered act. 'Kill who?'

'People.'

'What people?'

'Just people. Nobodies. You won't even know their names.'

Doyle gave no answer. He sat erect now, face set, just looking straight ahead.

Ferris gave him a few moments. Then he pulled the car over to the kerb and stopped. He pulled the handbrake on.

He reached across Doyle and opened the door.

'If you can't stand the heat, son, get out of the kitchen.'

Still Doyle kept up the impression of a man deeply considering the implications. Ferris watched him closely.

Finally Doyle made up his mind.

He reached out and slammed the door shut.

The small feral smile widening Ferris's mouth that dinted in the plump cheeks abruptly vanished. Now he was deadly serious.

'Extermination,' he said. 'That's what it's all about. We kill to order.'

Ferris drove out to an isolated stretch of waste ground

where, now and again, rusty lorries drove up to dump refuse even the municipal rubbish dumps wouldn't take.

Tall chimneys punctured the horizon, the mud and greasy pools glistened in sunshine, and piles of rubbish mouldered away. Doyle hefted the Walther PPK, took aim at a rusty tin can, and pressed the trigger.

The bullet struck a spout of gluey mud a foot or so to the right of the tin. The smell lifted, thick and tongue-coating. Ferris watched, standing to one side and to the rear of the man with the gun.

Doyle shot again, sending a quick succession of shots into the tin can, making it skip across the mud.

Ferris nodded to himself, chewing chocolate, and wandered over to Doyle. He took the pistol from Doyle's hand.

'You're good.'

'You didn't tell me it pulled to the right.'

The small fat smile indicated Ferris was impressed.

Doyle didn't mention that no one much used Walther PPKs on this side of the Channel after that fiasco when a royal kidnap had nearly gone through. The smells from the stagnant pools were getting to him. In all probability if he slipped and stuck his foot into a miniature lake of gunk the acids would chew his shoe away and probably strip his flesh to the bone like a pack of inanimate piranha. He followed Ferris over to the car.

'Come on,' said Ferris, leading the way.

'Where now?'

'Told you,' said Ferris, climbing in. 'The man wants to meet you.'

The two men spoke little on the way back to town, and Doyle was perfectly content about that. He had, he felt sure, passed the shooting test as he had the first run around. This man Ferris spoke of was the man Doyle wanted to meet. They eased gently through the thickening traffic, turning and twisting along side roads, to pull up beside a brick wall flanking a gaunt factory building. There were vestiges of blue sky to be glimpsed between the tall walls and gantries, the loading bays and serried windows. Very little activity was in progress. The place held a decayed and unused air.

The sliding door was opened by Ferris with a heave and a grunt and he and Doyle stepped through into the shadows of the factory floor. Dust stung Doyle's nostrils. Rack after rack of clothes cluttered the sides, and at the far end a ricketty staircase led up to a couple of glass-fronted offices on a higher level, overlooking the floor. From up there, no doubt, the bosses kept beady eyes fastened on the workers below.

Then his attention was taken by something else.

A small TV camera, hitched to a bracket, peered down with its single polished eye. It seemed to Doyle to be a modern continuation of the observation kept on this place when the factory had been working, for Ferris said: 'The company went bankrupt. We bought it up cheap.'

The cable from the TV camera led up into one of the offices.

Doyle was willing to bet that TV camera was an addition by the man Ferris had mentioned.

Towards the centre rear, below the elevated offices, lay an open space between the racked clothes. Here a few old benches stood, rooted to the floor, tiredly bearing ancient sewing machines. By their look of dust and neglect they had not been used for some time.

Sitting on one of the benches a man in his late twenties, broad of shoulder and with quick, dark eyes, sized Doyle up. He sat negligently, swinging one polished shoe. But he looked powerful and possessed of a dark inner knowledge of his own worth.

Ferris waved a hand in greeting.

'Hello, doc. Got another one for you.'

So this was the medical, Doyle was reasoning out. The man, whose name was Twig, stood up slowly. With careful, almost finicky movements, he took off his coat and placed it on one of the many empty hangers swinging from the nearby racks. He gave the coat a careful pull to get the shape just right. Then, gently, he began to amble towards Doyle.

Somehow, Doyle rapidly lost the feeling that this man was a doctor, about to give him a medical.

'What's going on?'

Ferris looked self-satisfied.

'It's a medical.'

Twig lifted the fingers of his right hand and splayed them out. Then he clenched them into a fist. That fist looked knobby and hard and exceedingly unpleasant.

'Just,' said Twig. 'Just want to check you over. Make sure you're fit.'

Ferris sniggered.

'His legs are all right. He can run.'

He sat back on a bench, making himself comfortable, all set to enjoy the coming fight.

The broad-shouldered young man with his white shirt very pronounced against the smart tailoring of his waistcoat bored in. He wasted no time. He feinted left and then let rip a snorting blow at Doyle's head.

Ray Doyle was not at all keen in getting into a roughhouse.

He ducked away, slipping the blow, moving back with deceptive ease.

Twig followed up. He put in a few exploratory jabs and then feinted again. Doyle remained content to fend the fellow off. But Twig was useful. He feinted again, and then used it as the old one-two. His right fist sank into Doyle's stomach.

Doyle collapsed. He fell down. And he stayed down.

Breathing lightly, fists raised, Twig looked down.

Ferris, in a casual almost uninterested way, said: 'Problem?'

'Yeah,' said Twig. 'Our friend here could have a problem. The medical term is lack of bottle.'

Slowly, Doyle rose to his feet. He looked warily at Twig. That gentleman pulled his waistcoat down and sneered.

If they'd been content to leave it at that, all well and

good. As it was, Twig came in again, hard, pushy, quite clearly determined to give this jumped-up specimen of a recruit before him a good thrashing. He battered at Doyle.

The ex-policeman blocked the first blows. His guts still ached where Twig had hit him. Almost without having to think about it, he avoided the onslaught and let rip with a few counter-punches. He caught Twig in the ribcage, dropped one in a little lower, heard Twig grunt, and then clipped him across the jaw. Twig staggered back.

The only sounds were those of the slide and stamp of feet, the ragged indrawn breathing, the thud of fists striking home. Doyle smashed Twig across the face, belted him in the guts. He bored on, got Twig retreating, hit him again and followed up. He wanted to get this ugly scene over with as quickly as possible. He moved on now with deadly purpose.

Ferris stuck out an elegant shoe and his leg tripped Doyle. Doyle went sprawling, carried on by his own momentum.

When he climbed back to his feet his face showed the other two that now he meant business.

Ferris's throat went dry.

Twig looked about in panic.

He snatched up a length of lumber lying across a bench. He cocked it in his fists, slanting up, shining, ready to bash Doyle's brains out.

He stalked forward. Now it was Doyle's turn to back off.

A damned stupid clothes rack got in the way and Doyle tripped. He half-stumbled and staggered. He caught a glimpse of Twig, face inflamed, lifting the length of wood high, high . . .

The voice of Brown Bear Doyle had heard over the phone cut in. It spoke calmly, giving an order to which it expected instant obedience.

'That's enough.'

Slowly, shoving the clothes rack out of the way, Doyle got to his feet.

The voice came from the office windows, one of them,

set up on their elevated platform. There was no sign of the speaker

'Pay him,' said the voice of Brown Bear, 'and take him out

For a moment Doyle did not move.

He felt anger and resentment. His guts ached. But he'd landed a few telling blows on this smart character, Twig, and if this was another test then it would appear he'd passed.

So he was ready to follow as Ferris led off to the door. He did not look back at Twig.

As he was about to go out, Ferris put a hand inside his jacket and produced a brown manilla envelope. He handed it across.

'We'll be in touch,' he said, as Doyle took the envelope.

Doyle nodded, and went out of the door. He took a deep breath. The door slid shut behind him. He looked around.

Then he slit the envelope open and looked inside.

Fivers, mostly, with a few tenners. About a hundred pounds' worth. Not bad for what had so far gone on. He stuffed the envelope full of money back into the pocket of his donkey jacket and strolled casually over to the low brick wall at the side of the mouldering factory. No one was about. He just hopped over the wall and ducked down, out of sight.

This was now his turn to make it an obbo job. Be nice to get that invisible man Doyle had dubbed Brown Bear running from phone box to phone box and then roughhouse with a young punk with delusions of grandeur. He rubbed his stomach. Punk.

That young punk, Twig, with the smart three-piece suit, was taking the jacket off the clothes rack and putting it on. The abandoned clothing factory smelled of dust and decay. Twig went across to one of the tables and found a clothes brush. He began to brush his jacket with loving care.

Ferris gave Twig a single glance, a mingled glance of wariness and contempt, and then stiffened up as the voice of the man reached him. Doyle might call this shadowy figure Brown Bear; Ferris called him 'the man', and the connotations of evil power in that simple name were enough to frighten subordinates.

'Well?' said the disembodied voice from the offices on their platform. The man must be using a mike.

Ferris said at once, speaking in something of a gabble: 'He's not bad. In fact, I think he's pretty good. He's all right. 'Course, I could be wrong.'

The voice sounded weary.

'You have an evasive quality, Ferris, which I find – tiresome.'

'Evasive?'

The voice ignored the vacant repetition.

'What do you think of the man?'

'I think,' said Ferris, swallowing. 'I think he's suitable.'

'Fortunately we do not have to rely on your powers of judgement. In my opinion, he could well be a plant.'

Ferris glanced at Twig, disturbed. That elegant young man, absorbed by a speck of lint around his left elbow, merely moved his shoulders, a kind of shrug which said he wasn't going to commit himself. He wasn't being paid to think about the patients' credentials. He was being paid to fight the patients and discover their quality and their bottle.

'Follow him,' ordered the voice. 'Check him, and if I'm right, you know what to do.'

'Right,' said Ferris, dutifully.

'I'm leaving now. Give me five minutes.'

This session was at an end.

Outside behind his brick wall Doyle stretched cautiously. Keeping an obbo tended to stiffen up the old joints if you didn't flex them occasionally; and if flexing your body meant you would be observed, then, simply – you did not flex. He heard the sound of a car's starter motor from the rear of the building, and then the burst of power as the motor caught on choke and a trifle too much throttle.

Immediately he belted off towards the back. He was only one pair of eyes and one pair of legs, and he couldn't be in two places at once.

He pelted around the corner of the factory in time to see

the tail end of a car passing beyond a far wall. The car's exhaust belched blue smoke, corroboration of the too enthusiastic use of the choke and accelerator theory. The car was gone. Doyle looked annoyed.

There was no sense hanging about here. He started off back to the front of the factory, past the filthy windows and the air outlets in rusty sheet metal, and the discarded boxes and twisted hangers. As he reached the corner where the low brick wall joined he heard voices and saw Ferris and Twig walking out of the door.

Doyle ducked down out of sight.

Ferris was saying: 'We just do as we're told. Right?'

Twig didn't answer the order directly.

'But who is he?'

'How should I know?' Ferris started to strip the paper and foil from a chocolate bar. He sounded confident. 'He pays the money, that's all we've got to worry about.'

They walked away and the rumble of their voices was lost to Doyle crouched behind his wall.

When they had gone he stood up and walked slowly along trying to figure out the angles. He felt pretty confident he had passed the tests. But if Ferris and Twig didn't know who they were working for, Doyle had a long long way to go before he got to the heart of the problem.

The van had once been a smaller breed of pantechnicon. If you looked hard enough you could find traces of heavily ornate painted lettering beneath the overall coat of green paint the shop had slapped on. The letters spelled out something something and Sons Ltd. That had been a good long time ago. Now the side of the van had been cut out, a flap counter fitted below and a folding shutter above. The tea urn, simmering and chuckling away, bore just the right number of dents and scratches on its polished rotundity. The plates were still china, as were the cups and saucers, thick, white, institutional china. Added an air of verisimilitude to the job, that thick white china, that no amount of fancy plastic or compressed paper cups could ever give.

Stan, wearing a striped apron in blue and white, stood behind the counter. There were a few buns and doughnuts under covers, and the sugar was still loose in bowls. More local colour.

Stan, somehow, did not quite fit the impression you felt you ought to take of a tea-bar proprietor. He might call it a snack bar and offer coffee as well; but you knew what you expected. Stan looked hard, with a ridged face and he moved with the lithe grace of a boxer.

Ray Doyle slouched along the pavement, out of the way of the passing traffic. The mobile tea van ahead, what the lads called the mobile snack bar, wisped its steam and Doyle rather fancied a cuppa. His hands were dug down into the pockets of his donkey jacket. Lorries and cars passed in an endless stream, and, occasionally, a lorry would pull off into the layby to stop and disgorge a hairy-chested driver with a thirst.

Doyle walked up and leaned on the flap counter.

As he leaned so he gave a casual swift glance back.

Yes. Ferris was still trailing him. Doyle had made no attempt to shake the tail off. He just made sure Ferris was not in earshot.

'Tea,' said Doyle. 'No sugar.'

Stan picked up a cup, inspected it critically, held it under the spout of the urn. Beautiful golden liquid gushed. Steam rose.

Doyle handed a few coins across as the cup, plus milk and minus sugar, was placed on the counter.

'I want a meet with Cowley. Here. In an hour.'

He spoke so that Stan could hear, lifting the cup to his lips so as to cover their movement from Ferris's gaze.

Then, in his normal voice, taking a sip and grimacing, he said: 'What d'you use to make this? Seaweed?'

Stan looked thunder, as much as to say that he didn't join CI5 to serve tea and when he did he didn't serve it to be sneered at by other jumped-up CI5 agents.

Instead of thick white china, it was thin and elegant bone china. Instead of solid tea it was rarefied coffee. Nigel

Dawson, in his late thirties and with a sharp mind, sipped the coffee and watched the man with the billiards cue at the snooker table. This was an exclusive, a refined, an opulent and an expensive – a very expense-account expensive – London Club. Although men on expense accounts, somehow, didn't seem to fit in with the establishment clientele. It was all in the way you phrased it, the way you looked at it.

This club appeared to be all deep leather armchairs, the right newspapers, potted palms, padding and obsequious waiters and a deathly hush.

You could, though, talk in the billiards room.

The snooker player struck irritably at the white, miscued, and neatly put it into the green pocket. He was around fifty years of age, handsome in a florid way, determined, and – an admission he let slip now and then – still ambitious enough to believe that, one day, he could become PM.

'Cowley's late,' he said, consulting his watch, the cue spearing dangerously.

Dawson uncrossed his elegant legs and recrossed them.

'The traffic perhaps.'

'We managed to get here on time.'

Dawson picked up the Minister's cup from the side table.

'More coffee, sir?'

'Thank you.' As Dawson fussed with the coffee things, the Minister went on: 'How's Charles?'

'A little better, I understand.'

The billiards cue waved. 'Are you coping?'

Dawson handed the coffee across. 'I think so.'

'I'm sure you are.'

Nigel Dawson's thin and aristocratic face, rather on the pale side, reflected nothing of the thoughts in his sharp mind. He had been most careful to wear his old school tie to this meeting with the Minister and George Cowley. The Minister was wearing an old school tie. It was the same as that gracing the neck of Nigel Dawson. These little things, particularly in this kind of atmosphere, mattered . . .

Sipping his coffee, the billiards cue laid decently to rest, the Minister leaned forward. He spoke in a confidential tone, conveying profound meanings that were transparently clear.

'Tell me, Nigel. Could you run MI6 on a permanent basis?'

Dawson had fielded plenty of those trick questions before. The candidate will act in a proper fashion . . . Oh, yes, he was up to that elementary manoeuvring.

In a smooth voice, he said: 'I think, as Sir Charles's deputy, perhaps the question would be better put to him.'

The Minister leaned back. He conveyed the sense of being pleased with the answer. Just another of the surface cat-and-mouse, the expected response. Both men were perfectly aware of the hunger for power burning in them both. They merely acted out the conventions required by their class and position.

The Minister, still with that smug expression on his face, saw George Cowley hurrying past the further billiards table and approaching with his determined limping walk.

'At last!'

Cowley limped up. 'Minister, Dawson. Sorry I'm late.'

The Minister favoured Cowley with a cold look. This fellow George Cowley was not quite out of the right hat, and he was notorious for his determination. In Criminal Intelligence Five, Cowley controlled an organisation of immense, if vague, powers. Formed to combat organised crime with the methods Cowley had developed at MI5, CI5, often called the Squad, or the Big A, found itself called in to handle a bewildering variety of crimes, villains and spies, traitors and their ilk. Anything working against the good of the country in the widest sense was grist to Cowley's mill at CI5.

The small print on the contract said so.

'Well,' said the Minister. 'Let's get on with it.'

From his briefcase he extracted two copies of a typed report. The covers contained a slim file each. He handed one to Dawson, the other to Cowley.

'These are the proposed financial cuts.'

Cowley flipped the cover open, skimmed through rapidly, picking out the salient points, seeing the diabolical figures leap out at him. This was the surgeon's knife at the throat and heart of his organisation. This was potentially lethal. He controlled himself. His sandy hair caught the overhead lighting and glinted, and his lined, handsome face, heavy now with power and responsibilities, showed clearly the struggle he was having.

The Minister said: 'Before you start arguing, Cowley, the cuts are mandatory.'

'I thought you said proposed.'

'You must try to master Whitehall jargon. I'll expect your reports on how to plan to implement the cuts within a week.'

Nigel Dawson's smooth: 'Yes, sir,' echoed into the silence.

The Minister looked at Cowley. The florid face tinged with heightened colour. 'Cowley?'

'I'll do my best.'

It was not quite a surly answer, and Cowley cast a veiled glare at Dawson, who was clearly lapping up the situation.

The Minister went on speaking. 'Now, item two, security. After recent unfortunate events, I think the overall picture is satisfactory.'

Cowley said: 'I'm afraid I don't.' Now his voice was plummy, the trace of a northern accent completely overlaid by his ability to express what he wanted to say succinctly.

The Minister raised his eyebrows. 'Really.'

Cowley took his heavy glasses off and folded them. It was a gesture that held their attention on him and what he was saying. 'We never seem to learn. Every few months some new mole, some double agent, some new scandal is uncovered. Everyone gets excited, the papers are full of it and then the dust settles.'

The Minister said: 'Go on,' as Cowley paused.

'Then,' said George Cowley, 'Then we go back to the

same smug, complacent attitude I'm hearing here today. I'm sorry, Minister. I consider the security situation is far from satisfactory.'

Quite evidently the Minister did not at all like what he was hearing. Nigel Dawson eased himself back into the conversation with what ought to have been a torpedo in the guts for the head of CI5.

'What would you propose we do?'

Cowley shook his head with conviction. 'No matter what it takes, no matter how much dirt we uncover, why don't we purge our Intelligence Services clean, once and for all?'

'You're recommending a strong purgative for all of us,' said Dawson in a joking way, 'are you, George?'

'Don't get clever with me, Dawson. I'm serious.'

'Then I must take you seriously.'

The two men locked gazes and into that moment of sudden crisis a waiter padded up on shuffling waiter's feet. He put a phone extension down on the table, plugged it into the outlet conveniently situated for this kind of arrangement, and lifted the receiver.

The Minister just took the phone without a word of thanks and snapped into the mouthpiece. 'Yes?'

He was not pleased to discover the call was not for him but for George Cowley.

Cowley walked around the table and took the phone.

'Cowley . . . Right . . . I'm on my way.'

He put the receiver back on its cradle.

'I'm sorry but I'm afraid I have to leave.' He nodded to the Minister and to Dawson, two stiff little jerks of that sandy head, and walked abruptly away. He walked in a very upright posture, his immaculate coat fitting perfectly; but he still limped. That Condor Legion bullet he'd picked up in Spain still nestled in his leg. It gave him hell from time to time, and the doctors had told him that if they tried to remove it there was an overwhelming chance he'd lose the leg altogether. So George Cowley limped.

The Minister and Dawson looked after him as he passed the billiards table and went out of that elegant room

'Extraordinary,' said the Minister. 'Didn't even touch his coffee.'

'Obviously a busy man.'

'So are we all.' The quick response was followed by a slight pause in which what the Minister had to say gained in importance. Then: 'A frank opinion, Nigel. Off the record.'

'Of what, sir?'

'George Cowley.'

Dawson spoke slowly, as though caught unprepared. He had long since formed an opinion of Cowley, and now he trotted it out suitably attired in the regalia of privileged information.

'Well . . . Impulsive, headstrong. Perhaps too independent, too powerful. Not accountable enough to the right people.'

'Not a team man.'

'No, sir.'

The Minister sighed. 'Not my sort, I'm afraid.'

'Not *our* sort, sir.'

'Indeed.'

Again the Minister let the conversation flow along without spoken words. Both men knew exactly what they were doing. Then, and with some reluctance, the Minister said: 'Of course, he's highly thought of.'

'Yes. I understand the PM looks on Cowley very favourably.'

'He would make a dangerous enemy.'

'For you, sir?'

The smell of coffee mingled with the lingering dusty smell of cue chalk hung in the air. The Minister stood up, brushing his trouser legs.

'For either of us.' He half-turned. 'Can I give you a lift?'

Dawson was in there like a ferret after a rabbit.

'Thank you.'

The potentialities of their conversation went with them in each man's thoughts as they left the club and were carried in the Minister's limousine towards Whitehall. The

Minister leaned forward and slid the glass partition up sealing off the driver. This was a small, habitual action of secrecy, not remarked on. He did not turn to regard Dawson fully; but Dawson was well aware that the Minister was observing him.

'If,' said the Minister. 'If I did cross swords with Cowley – for whatever reason – '

'Would it ever come to that?'

'It might. In such a confrontation, where would you stand, Nigel?'

The answer poured out like liquid sunshine.

'You could rely on my discretion and complete support, sir.'

The Minister nodded, satisfied to leave the question, for the moment, at that.

Before he returned to the mobile snack bar to meet Cowley – for the meet with Cowley was the current jargon – Doyle had to throw Ferris off his tail. Ferris stuck like glue. Doyle managed to do it by leading Ferris through a loading area where vans were being filled with cardboard boxes from the stores. Come to think of it, the vans could be in process of being emptied; no activity was going on and no cardboard boxes moved into or out of a van.

Ferris came pattering into the area, saw Doyle angle past the bonnet of a red-painted van, and followed. He waited a moment by the cab of the van, resting against the shiny red paint. When he looked around he expected to see Doyle just about to reach the far corner. Ferris was surprised.

No Doyle.

There was no way Doyle could have gone into the doorway from the nearest stores entrance. Ferris looked around. Then he went back and lifted the rear doors of the van and looked inside. He even went so far as to knock a few of the cardboard boxes about, most unpleasantly, to see if Doyle was hiding behind them. Still no Doyle. Ferris moved off to the side and, suddenly, quickly, looked under the van.

No Doyle.

Ferris realised that Doyle, who knew how to run, give him that, must have put his head down and fairly sprinted for the far corner past the shops. Ferris cursed, both Doyle and himself, and started running for the corner.

When the sound of his footfalls faded, Doyle stood up on the roof of the van, jumped down to that red-painted bonnet, and from thence to the concrete of the loading area.

He sauntered off, hands stuck down into the pockets of his donkey jacket.

Traffic passed and repassed as Doyle ambled along to the layby where the mobile snack bar still puffed glistening steam, and Stan still served terrible tea. There was no sign of Cowley; but his car was parked at the extreme end of the layby. Doyle noticed.

'Tea,' he told Stan. Then he caught a remembrance of the taste of the tea, a real Proustian remembrance, and he pulled a face and added quickly: 'Make that coffee.'

He leaned on the flap counter as Stan began operations to produce a liquid he called coffee. Cowley was sitting on a box in the space behind the bar, looking up with his lips twisting in that famous Cowley grimace that meant either you'd dropped a most godawful brick, or he was having you shot.

'I left an important meeting to come here, Doyle. Why couldn't you phone in?'

'I had a tail.'

'Are you still being followed?'

Doyle sipped the coffee, looking back with a single comprehensive glance. 'No, I think he's given up, like this coffee.'

'What have you got?'

'Well, they're recruiting assassins ready to kill for money.'

'Who are the targets?'

'I don't know – except the contact said they were nobodies.'

George Cowley ruminated on that one. 'Why kill people

of no importance?' He looked up as Doyle pushed the coffee cup aside, the coffee was worse than the tea, as usual, and waited for the vile stuff to slop onto him. When he was safe, he went on: 'Any idea who's behind it?'

'Well, the top man was there. But he kept out of sight.'

'I see.'

Doyle was anxious to get this assignment over with. For obvious reasons.

'Do we close in?'

'No. Not yet.'

Doyle moved his shoulders in the donkey jacket. Well, he hadn't expected anything else, really. 'Right. I'll report tomorrow.'

When one of his two top agents had walked off, Cowley took out his R/T and got onto the other half of the partnership.

'This is Cowley,' he said in clear into the mouthpiece. Callsigns would follow if it got rough. 'Where's Bodie?'

'At the rendezvous, sir,' came the answer.

'Right. Stay with him.'

Not without a little stab of pain from that damned leg, Cowley hauled himself up and out the back way of the van. When Stan went to help, Cowley gave him a look. That look said, *inter alia:* 'D'you think I'm an old man, then? You're wrong.'

Bodie looked smart, hard, trim. You might want to call Bodie dapper; but you might end up with a bunch of fives parting your ivories. Yes, he was a hard, dark man, Bodie. He was one of those lucky guys who can drape clothes and always look good. He'd been through the Paras and the mercenaries and the smugglers and – you name it. If Bodie hadn't done it he knew someone who had. And now he worked for CI5 and was teamed up with Ray Doyle, the ex-copper. Doyle was a good egg; but Bodie wouldn't tell him that. They'd laid their own lives on the line for their partner's – more than once.

Now Bodie stood easily in the doorway, rather like that famous tiger at the waterhole, watching the pair of phone boxes opposite. Williams paced up and down outside, looking nervous. Williams had checked the phone box, just as Doyle had done, and now he waited, pacing up and down. He was around thirty or so, with a round boyish face and fair hair. He ran his hand through his hair, and took another turn up and down.

Bodie looked back at the CI5 car parked at the kerb with Pocock at the wheel. Pocock, big and husky, gave a nod to indicate he was still awake. Bodie nodded back and crossed the road to the phone boxes. He tossed a couple of coins in his hand, ignored Williams, went in and dialled out the number.

Williams was just checking his watch for the umpteenth time when the phone in the nearest box rang. He dived in and scooped up the receiver.

'Hello . . .'

Bodie took the phone from his ear, looked at it, looked through the glass at the other box, and realised just what he had done. That famous Bodie wrinkle crinkled up his lips. He put the phone down, gently, leaned around to the next box, and said, brightly: 'Hello!'

Williams said 'Hello.' He was still speaking into the phone.

'Right,' said Bodie in that bright, cheerful, infuriating way, 'here.'

Williams spun about as though a giant spider had sneaked up and tapped him on the shoulder.

'Wha? – Who are you?'

'I was going to ask you the same question.'

'I don't understand.'

Bodie sighed. 'Let me take a guess. You were told to wait here for a call, right?'

Williams did not answer.

'I,' Bodie said, 'was told to come here and make a call.'

To the CI5 agent's surprise, the first reaction was not followed by the expected second reaction on Williams' part, for he simply pushed past out of the phone kiosk, completely ignoring Bodie. Bodie grabbed his arm.

Williams said, quickly: 'I don't know what you're talking about.'

The bruising on the man's face was recent, shiny, and plum-coloured.

'Had a medical recently?' Bodie realised that the man was still unsure, and pressed on. 'They wanted us to meet.'

The facts in the case were obvious, and once Williams was over his first and very natural suspicions, he and Bodie could take a stroll in the nearby park and get down to business.

'When I first got involved,' Williams told Bodie. 'I thought they were recruiting mercenaries. For Africa or somewhere.'

'Yeah,' said Bodie. He knew all about mercenaries in Africa, did Bodie.

'If I'd known then –'

'But you needed the money.' Bodie knew he'd hit the nail on the head as Williams didn't answer. 'What's her name?'

'Who?'

'The girl you need the money for.'

The round face clouded. 'Get lost.'

Williams started to walk off. Bodie had to act fast. He pulled Williams back, easily, and said: 'Take it easy. With me, it's the gee-gees. Can't leave them alone.' Williams looked mollified, and Bodie went on: 'What did they tell you?'

'They told me nothing. They gave me a ticket.'

'Yeah, well,' Bodie said. 'They told me where to take the ticket.'

Whoever was running this outfit, they had a security system all neatly worked out. Williams and Bodie went to the left luggage office, where the rush of people to and from the trains eddied about them. The smell of dust and many people hung in the air; only diesel exhaust stank now, there was no heady aroma of steam. The CI5 car with Pocock at the wheel tooled into the waiting bay.

Pocock got out and went into a side door marked STAFF ONLY.

Williams gave Bodie the left luggage ticket and, moving slowly, Bodie went across to the counter. The attendant in his white-piped grey coat took the ticket and shuffled off to the racks at the rear. He went around the corner out of sight. Bodie leaned on the counter and Williams joined him.

In the safe area at the rear the attendant matched the ticket with the other half on a brown canvas holdall. With a grunt and a heave he hauled it out, and Pocock came through the side door from the staff entrance holding out his CI5 identification.

As the attendant gaped, Pocock went efficiently to work.

He checked the contents of the holdall. There were two brown manila envelopes and a set of car keys. He opened the first envelope and pursed his lips at the glossy photograph and the sheet of typewritten instructions. He knew what this was, all right. He took out his miniature camera, put it to his eye and started to take shots of the contents of the canvas holdall.

Leaning on the counter outside, fretfully, Williams said in his half-whining manner: 'What's the hold up?'

Bodie didn't bother to answer.

After a time in which Bodie just acted as though there was no hold up at all, the attendant came out of the rear safe area. When Williams started to open the bag, Bodie stopped him.

'Not here.'

He picked up the holdall and marched off.

Williams, looking uncertain again, had to follow.

As they left the station Bodie glanced casually at the CI5 car. Back behind the wheel, Pocock gave a little nod – All well.

The spot they chose in the park was deserted except for a girl in jeans and shirt who walked away around the flowering shrubs. Bodie and Williams sat on a park bench and opened the holdall. They took an envelope each.

Williams' envelope was full of money. It looked to be a lot of money in neat one thousand packs. Excitedly, he began to count the cash.

Bodie looked sombrely at the photograph from the other envelope. He held the typed instructions angled and did not look at them, just at the photo.

'What's that?' said Williams, hands full of money.

'The target. The woman we kill for the ten thousand.'

Williams' smile faded, and his nervousness returned.

They studied the glossy photograph.

The face was only slightly lined, a square yet alive face, the lips curved in a smile. The hair was not yet fully grey. Bodie put her down at around fifty. She looked comfortable, happy, the sort of woman who could hold down a job with one hand. Somehow he got the impression out of his experience of life that she was unmarried.

He tossed the car keys in his hand, looking at the photograph of the woman they'd been paid ten thousand pounds to kill.

Then he checked the address written on the label tied to the car keys. He looked at Williams.

'Let's go.'

Bodie did not like this one, at all. This one smelled bad – nasty and bad.

They found the car parked at the address, tucked away in the side street. The key fitted the driver's door. Bodie got in, and leaning across opened the door for Williams.

The car was an ordinary, plain, unadorned Escort, the kind of car that would attract no unwelcome attention. Bodie looked at the typewritten instructions.

'Check the glove compartment.'

Obediently, Williams did so. He took out the gun very gingerly, holding it by the barrel. Bodie took it from him and, nonchalantly, with an inhalation of breath, stuck it down his belt. It was a Walther PPK

Uneasily, Williams said: 'We could take the money and run.'

Bodie started up the car.

'How far would we get?'

He started off, eased out of the side street and joined the flow of traffic. They were on their way to the address of the woman in the photograph, on their way to murder her.

She lived in a bungalow at the end of a quiet lane in an isolated and peaceful spot. The Dawn Chorus would have all the space to sing here of a morning. It was very quiet. Here the woman had come to retire and get away from it all.

When Bodie pulled the car in and switched off the engine, Williams was quite clearly even more apprehensive.

Jerking his thumb at the bungalow, just visible beyond the hedge, Bodie said: 'That must be it.'

He took the Walther from his belt, pulled out the magazine to check it and make sure – no theatrical piece of routine this but practical common-sense – and snapped it back. Williams recoiled at the hard metallic click.

He swallowed. 'This is crazy . . .' He saw Bodie handling the gun, playing with it, suddenly pointing it as though to shoot. 'I . . . I can't go through with it.'

That suited the CI5 agent.

'Stay here.'

He was out of the car and slamming his door – and then holding it so that it shut with a tiny click – before Williams could answer. He padded up the path.

He checked through the side windows and saw merely a kitchen and bedroom. The bungalow was not new, but it was not exactly old. Around the back French windows were unlocked. The crazy-paving underfoot might have made an incautious footfall echo; Bodie moved like a panther. He eased the windows open and stepped gently into the room.

The room was cluttered. Cluttered – it was jam-packed with oddments, junk, antiques, books and framed photographs. Here lay the remnants of a life, collected and cherished. Before the open fireplace stood two tall-backed chairs, a nice comfortable arrangement for chilly evenings.

Bodie moved soundlessly across the carpet, which was a little worn here and there. A photograph in a silver frame be an archaeologist's nightmare, or paradise depending on your point of view. Ferris and Twig lounged in that forlorn landscape as the man in the dirty mackintosh walked towards them.

He was around thirty, the usual useful age they liked to recruit, gaunt of face and angular of movement. He walked up with a look of expectation.

Ferris said, casually: 'How was Malta?'

The man's gaunt face twitched as a muscle jumped.

'All right.'

'We heard your man fell over a cliff.'

'He was walking too near the edge.'

Twig leaned on the jetty rail at the gaunt man's back, :leaning his nails with a file. The gaunt man, aware that Twig was there, did not turn around. He was looking with nterest at Ferris's right hand, which appeared from inside is coat bearing an envelope. These envelopes bore grief nd good news, depending on their contents.

'You've done well,' Ferris told the gaunt man.

The man held out his hand for the envelope, and Ferris, th a feral little smile, jerked his hand back. The man who d come back from Malta suddenly realised that Ferris sn't intending to part with the envelope.

Something was wrong . . .

The man was too late.

Twig reached for his raincoat and jerked it down over his ulders and halfway down his arms.

t once a frantic struggle began. But Twig just pushed man towards the edge of the jetty. The raincoat pered any defence and Twig upended the fellow and d him over.

fell, legs whirling, hit the mud.

rris and Twig leaned over, rather as Roman senators t lean to watch a particularly tasty bit of action in the . The man shrugged the mackintosh back on and o plunge through the mud towards the bank.

fell over. He was now a black mud-caked figure d for destruction. He floundered on, arms flailing,

on the jumbled sideboard caught his eye. He knew that heavy square face, that bulldog jaw, the big cigar. The autograph was bold and definite. Winston Churchill.

A voice, a woman's voice, said: 'Chartwell, 1953. It was nice of him to sign it for me, don't you think?'

Bodie turned without seeming to move. He was facing one of the high backed chairs, the one from which the woman's voice reached him. She was about ten years older than she'd been in the photograph he'd taken from the envelope. She was the target for murder. Miss Walsh was dressed in a tweed skirt and comfortable shoes. Her twin set was of some indeterminate beigey colour. She peered over the top of her spectacles, and pushed back an untidy strand of grey hair. Her general appearance, rather like a disturbed dormouse, gave her a slightly eccentric air.

'We've been waiting for you,' Miss Walsh said

Bodie said: 'We!'

A familiar plummy voice from the other chair said:

'Yes, Bodie. We.'

And George Cowley stood up from the highbacked chair.

The unlocked French windows were now fully explained. Pocock had done his job. Bodie felt relief that he had not been obliged to stall Miss Walsh until Cowley arrived.

The chief of CI5 said: 'Where's your accomplice?'

'Still in the car.'

Miss Walsh, with a little bounciness to her steps, most surprising and pleasant, went across to the sideboard and opened one of the doors. Half bent, she peered back and up. 'Can I offer you a drink?'

The men declined, so she poured herself a vodka and tonic. 'Well, young man. I don't suppose you'd like to tell me?'

'What's that, Miss Walsh?'

'Just exactly what is going on.'

Bodie looked under his eyebrows at Cowley, waiting for the chief to give the necessary clearance for explanations.

'It's all right. Elizabeth has security clearance. Among

other things, she was Under Secretary to the Cabinet Office.'

'Interesting job,' remarked Bodie in his bright bird-like Bodie way.

'Yes,' said Miss Walsh. 'It was. Well . . . ?'

Cowley did the explaining.

'CI5 are infiltrating a group. This is a group recruiting hard men ready to murder for money.' Cowley looked soberly at Elizabeth Walsh. 'You are one of their targets. Bodie was sent here to kill you.'

He moved across to the window at the front and checked on the car which was just visible through the foliage. In the car Williams was wishing he could make a telephone call and guessing there wouldn't be a phone box within a quarter of a mile.

Cowley let the curtain drop and said: 'I'd think he'd be getting even more nervous by now. You'd better get on with it, Bodie.'

When the gun was drawn from Bodie's belt, Miss Walsh said: 'Ah – a Walther PPK.'

Politely, Bodie replied. 'You know your handguns, Miss Walsh.'

She took a flat black starting pistol from a drawer.

'Use this. I don't want an unsightly hole in the ceiling.'

Bodie played the pantomime through solemnly. After all, somebody wanted this woman dead. He pulled the trigger and the starting pistol cracked out. Bodie just went running hard down the garden path – Miss Walsh opened the front door for him – and belted into the car.

'Let's get moving!'

Williams stammered.

'Is she dead?'

'What do you think? Let's get out of here.'

The Cortina roared and drove recklessly along the quiet lane. Miss Walsh watched it go from the window and then turned to Cowley.

'It's an uncomfortable feeling, knowing someone wants to kill you.'

'It's also a problem.'

'Problem?'

'Why would anyone want to?'

'That had also crossed my mind,' said Miss Walsh. '
don't you tell me?'

'Tell you what?'

Miss Walsh revealed a little of the shrewdness that given her her job in the first place and kept her in successfully until she retired. 'The reason you're still and not rushing off somewhere putting the wor rights.'

Cowley smiled across at her and as she sat back in the chairs, he took the other. He had to phrase t right. But he thought he knew this woman's re would be the right ones.

'It's a tough one, Elizabeth, and I think it co tougher. There are loose ends, things that don't a need your help.'

'I'm retired, out of touch.'

'You're the cleverest woman I know.'

Miss Walsh reproved Cowley most mildly. must move in very limited circles.'

She finished her vodka and tonic.

Cowley shook his head, relishing the squat dering if he'd queered his pitch. But he wa serious as the men who wanted this woman de

'Will you help?'

'I,' said Miss Walsh, getting up and h sideboard, 'will think about it.'

Ferris stripped the wax paper from a p sweet and popped it into his mouth. Tha the only sweet thing around here. The mu was out and the mud extended in a flat from the jetty to the grey-green water's e

The disused jetty projected out ove decaying tooth into the river. The ancie stood in the black mud and what lay un

dragging one foot after the other.

Ferris nodded to Twig.

All the bets were down.

Twig drew his handgun and took careful aim.

He said: 'They kill for us. Then we kill them.'

'Yeah,' said Ferris, sucking on his sweet. 'It's a hard life.'

Twig fired.

The man reared and the mud dragged him down and he slumped. Face down into the slime, he fell. He did not attempt to rise again.

Ferris sucked on a bit of sweet caught in his tooth.

'One born every day of the week.'

His philosophy had been proved, perfectly and again.

Chapter Two

CI5 Headquarters were moved from place to place from time to time. Almost invariably the HQ would be set up in some shabby office block or warehouse complex, attracting no attention. Inside offices and facilities existed in a state that CI5 operatives had been known to describe as crummy. The forensic laboratory, the computer room and electronics, though, were always of the highest standard. The garage was always superbly equipped and right on top of the job.

Standing in the computer room, Cowley looked up as Elizabeth Walsh walked in. He went over at once to greet her.

'I'm glad you've decided to come.'

'You made it sound as though it could be interesting.'

Cowley smiled. 'I see your recent demise made *The Times.*'

'Yes,' said Miss Walsh brightly, peering over her spectacles. 'I found that encouraging.'

She carried a cavernous handbag, of the sort that might easily have concealed an Ernest Worthing, and Cowley took it from her and led her over to a desk. Above the desk a large notice board had been fixed to the wall.

Cowley put the handbag down on the desk and nodded to the notice board. The surface was blank except for the single photograph pinned up.

'Remember him?'

Miss Walsh looked, adjusting her gold-rimmed spectacles.

'Yes . . . Harris. Retired eight years ago and went to live in Malta.'

'I'm afraid he's dead.'

'Dead?'

'A cliff fall.'

The humming machinery and flickering lights of the computer room could not conceal the tension.

'Was,' said Miss Walsh. 'Was it an accident?'

'Perhaps.'

Cowley took a second photograph from the desk and pinned it up on the board. The pictured likeness of Miss Walsh looked out from the glossy surface.

'But you weren't an accident.'

From the desk drawer he took pins with vari-coloured heads, lengths of string also of different colours, and then a pile of small blank cards.

Miss Walsh looked on with the air of one who knew all about what she was seeing.

'You want me to work a puzzle board?'

'Who could do it better?'

Miss Walsh regarded Cowley with a look that could be construed as admonitory. She opened the handbag and without really having to look reached in and took out a half bottle of vodka.

'With that kind of brazen flattery I won't require this.' And she dropped the bottle in the waste paper basket at the side of the desk.

The CI5 computer operator, a charming young man with wavy fair hair and a winning smile, regarded Miss Walsh with some unease as she sailed up to him, rather like a Spanish carrack attempting to attack an English galleon.

'Young man,' said Miss Walsh in her grandest style. 'I need some files.'

'Do,' said the computer operator in a hushed voice, 'Do you have the magnetic tape references?'

She gave a little jerk of her thumb at the computer which effectively dismissed the electronic marvel.

'You won't find them in that infernal machine. These files will be encrusted with dust. The kind of files I like.'

Smiling benignly, Cowley started to walk away. The computer operator hurried after him.

'Does that woman have security clearance, sir?'

Cowley found it surprisingly pleasant to be able to answer. 'That woman was taking notes from Churchill when you were still wet behind the ears. Give her anything she wants.'

The Green Dragon Motel on a main highway leading out of London catered for a wide variety of tastes. If the occupant wished to remain practically invisible, that was his affair. Ferris drove into the forecourt of the motel, parked the car, and walked in past reception towards the accommodation. He checked numbers. When he found the right one he knocked and entered.

The room lay in semi-darkness, with a faint acrid odour on the air. The blinds were drawn across the windows and, suddenly, as Ferris entered the room, a brilliant flood of harsh light burst upon him.

He recoiled, automatically flinging up an arm to cover his eyes. A battery of powerful flood lights positioned to illuminate anyone against the door concealed whoever sat in the darkness beyond them.

The voice of the man Ferris called 'the man' said: 'Close the door.' When the door clicked shut, the man said: 'Well?'

'The woman's dead.'

'And Nielson?'

'We paid him off.' Ferris smiled ferally. 'Dumped him in the river.'

'You find something amusing?'

Ferris swallowed, and his eyes watered anew.

'No. I'm sorry, guv.'

The accented voice did not change in intonation; but the chill hit Ferris.

'I am not your guv. I am the man who pays you to do certain tasks.'

Ferris shifted awkwardly on his feet.

'Right.'

He peered forward, trying to see the man behind the

battery of impenetrable light. He caught the sound of scratching, and suddenly realised that the man was crossing off names on a list. Ferris swallowed again.

The voice from the lights said: 'What about the man I saw yesterday?'

'The one who gave Twig trouble? I followed him most of the day.'

The voice from the invisible man carried a tiredness. 'You're not even a competent liar. You lost him.'

'Yeah, well, I'm sorry. But I'm a fair judge. He's okay.'

'You think so.' The man now sounded amused, and yet the amusement was of the order of a cat toying with a mouse. 'Fortunately I have more reliable sources of information. He is an infiltrator. A plant.'

'What?'

'Dispose of him immediately. Report tomorrow.'

Ferris nodded. 'Tomorrow. Right.'

His nod was more like a submissive bow. Ferris understood the chilling power of the man hidden behind the battery of floodlights. He went out and shut the door. At that, he was relieved to leave the presence of the man.

If there was one thing Ferris and Twig prided themselves on, it was their capacity to work as a team. They drove to the pub and spotted Doyle just as he was leaving. Ferris pulled the car into the kerb, and Twig got out, leaving the door open. Only a few people were about, and no one paid the car or the men any attention.

Twig hurried along and caught up with Doyle.

'Where you off to?'

Doyle turned and surveyed Twig the immaculate.

'I thought you'd forgotten.'

'How could I forget you?'

Ferris eased the car up and Twig, gesturing to the open door, said: 'Hop in.'

Doyle could not hesitate too long. He opened the rear door and, in that instant, Twig chopped him down savagely, shoved him across into the front seat and then leaped into the rear. Ferris gunned the engine and the car leaped away, Doyle unconscious on the front passenger seat, Ferris at the wheel, Twig hauling himself up on the back seat, and the rear door swinging crazily open.

The clothing factory looked just as run down and decayed as ever. Bodie strode briskly along between the racks and Williams trailed uncertainly along afterwards.

Ferris sat on a bench waiting for them, swinging one leg. He wadded up chocolate wrappings as they approached and flicked the foil away. He held out a hand.

'Where's the gun?'

'We dumped it.' Bodie spoke evenly, quietly.

Ferris eyed the pair of them with some suspicion.

Williams, nervously, said: 'That's what the instructions said.'

Ferris relaxed. 'Good.' He took two envelopes from the bench and handed them across. 'Here's the other half.'

If character or training came into it, Bodie didn't give a damn: Williams just put his envelope straight in his pocket, Bodie slit his open and had a look.

More money.

Ferris sucked a tooth.

'Got another job for you.'

Williams hunched his shoulders. 'What sort of job?'

'We're only in one business.' Ferris spoke with a quiet satisfaction at his job prospects.

Bodie, more grimly than he intended, said: 'When?'

Ferris smiled. 'Right now.'

He hopped off the bench and turned to face up to the windows of the offices on the elevated platform. He was enjoying this. He shouted up.

'Bring him down.'

Williams fidgeted nervously and Bodie just tilted his smooth dark head up a little to watch. A man appeared at the top of the steps with Twig right behind. The immaculate Twig held a pistol under Doyle's ear, and he prodded him along just as though Doyle was a steer at the end of the electric goad going to the slaughterhouse.

Which, in the view of Twig and Ferris, was exactly what he was.

Bodie's face resembled a poker, or a face of a gambler playing poker. He did not tremble a muscle. Twig forced Doyle down the steps, one at a time, and the pistol did not waver.

Ferris, idly, took a Walther PPK from his pocket.

He held it casually between Williams and Bodie.

'Who wants this?'

The smell of nervousness was not particularly strong on Williams; but he made no move to take the handgun. Bodie took it. He was minded to gun Twig down and then brace Ferris up hard for questioning. But there was Williams, who was an unknown quantity and who wanted to murder for money. And there was the mysterious man organising this. Most of all – there was Cowley. If Bodie did a heroic stunt now, George Cowley would crucify him for fouling up the investigation.

So Bodie held out his hand.

'I'll do it.'

'I bet you would.' Ferris smiled his feral smile. 'I bet it was you who shot the old girl.' He prodded the gun towards Williams; 'Let's see you in action, son.'

A pink tongue flicked Williams' lips, and now Bodie caught the whiff of apprehension.

'You want me to do it here?'

'Here and now.'

During this, Doyle remained impassive and unmoving. The play was with his partner, and Bodie would do the right thing – in the end, and perhaps for the wrong reasons. Doyle had sweated out a few with Master Bodie.

As Twig folded his arms in expectation, but still kept his gun at the ready, Williams took the Walther PPK and walked slowly over to Doyle. Bodie watched. Williams pointed the gun at Doyle.

The gun wavered only a little, a tremble that would not be enough to make the bullet miss. At this pointblank range Williams couldn't miss.

Bodie flexed his shoulders inside his coat, and looked at Doyle, who gazed calmly back, the marks on his face pronounced in the shadowed lighting. Bodie looked up.

'What are you waiting for?' demanded Ferris.

Bodie said: 'Not here.'

Ferris swung around, glaring. Before he could speak, Bodie pointed up.

'Not with that camera up there.'

In that moment of perilous hesitation, as Ferris considered, and Williams trembled, and Bodie looked grim, Twig uncoiled his arms and his gun snouted, ready for instant action. At last Ferris relaxed.

'The man's careful. I like that. All right. Not here. But you keep the gun, and you – ' he pointed a jabbing finger at Williams. 'You do it!'

They used the same car to drive to the spot in the woods selected. Bodie could not help reflecting that Doyle must be imagining all kinds of interesting outcomes. He was, in the idiom of the 1920s, taking a ride.

Doyle was wondering just what Bodie was going to do that would not foul up the investigation.

The woods breathed a peacefulness over the scene that was brutally shattered as Williams pointed the gun at Doyle.

Twigs crunched underfoot, the smell of leafmould came surprisingly fresh, the light lay green and muted. No one would ever know a murder had been committed here.

Bodie held out his hand.

'You'd better give me the gun.'

Williams shook his head.

The negative was most positive.

Bodie just gave a little shrug and walked across to sit on a tree stump.

Doyle looked hard at his partner.

Bodie just sat.

Williams pointed the gun and Doyle began to move sideways. He circled warily, and as he circled so Williams turned on the spot, keeping the gun centred on Doyle's stomach.

The sweet warm woodland smells reached up.

It was very quiet.

Doyle circled and the muzzle of the gun remained pointing at his guts, and it was getting to be not at all funny.

Bodie just sat.

Doyle circled and turned Williams so that the man with the gun at last had his back to Bodie.

Doyle waited, no longer circling, feeling something remarkably like a red-hot poker investigating his inward parts.

What the hell was Bodie playing at?

The Walther PPK was no longer trembling. It held centred on Doyle. Williams appeared just about ready to shoot.

Bodie, silently, stood up and moved across. The ironhard edge of his hand crashed down onto Williams' wrist. The gun spun away to fall with a plop into leaf-mould. Williams leaped back, holding his wrist.

With fastidious attention, Bodie flicked bits of brown sticky leaf off the gun. He held it ready to shoot at once, if the need arose.

Doyle let out a breath.

He spoke in a sarcastic tone of voice, the tone of voice that would take the skin off a rhinoceros.

'Thank you.'

Bodie's skin was far tougher than any covering a rhinoceros could afford.

'For what?'

'For cutting it so fine.'

'I knew he couldn't do it.'

Bodie spoke casually, supremely confident in his judgement.

Doyle, on an inhalation, said: 'You knew that.'

'He's not the type.'

When Williams spoke, his voice and manner were

markedly different from the pose he had adopted previously. Suddenly, he looked a lot tougher.

'What the hell's going on? Who are you?'

Doyle said: 'Tell him.'

'You tell him.'

The partners could play this, like tennis, for as long as it amused them. They didn't like people who went around with the intention of murdering for money.

'We,' Doyle told the would-be assassin, 'are CI5.'

The emotion that fleeted across Williams' face was surprise; but he concealed it well.

'Show me your ID.'

'We're not carrying any ID. We're undercover.'

'Undercover.' Williams showed what he thought of that. He held out his hand for the gun. 'May I?'

Bodie glanced at Doyle, who looked ready to trust his maniac of a partner in this development. Bodie handed the Walther PPK across.

Now when Bodie chopped the edge of his hand down across a fellow's wrist, that same fellow was not going to do a lot with the hand on the end of the wrist for some time. Williams handled the gun with his left hand. And that made the demonstration that more impressive.

He spun about and triggered a rapid accurate burst of fire into a tree stump. The yellow wood splintered and flew. The cracks echoed in the woods. The smell of cordite drifted under the trees.

Williams breathed in deeply. He handed the gun back to Bodie.

'I'm undercover, too. I'm Williams – MI6.'

George Cowley crashed into Nigel Dawson's office with the finesse of a bulldozer entering a china shop with blade at the ready. He glared redly at Dawson, sitting calmly at the ornate desk.

'All right, Dawson. I want answers, and I want them now.'

Dawson very pointedly spoke past Cowley to his

secretary hovering in the doorway.

'It's all right, Miss Davis. Close the door, will you.' When Miss Davis withdrew, Dawson went on: 'I assume you have an explanation, Cowley, for bursting in here like an enraged bull?'

'Why didn't you tell me about Williams?'

'Williams?'

'Don't try that little boy lost look on me.'

'Ah, yes, Williams. He's been operating covertly. Undercover, as they say.'

Dawson's urbane manner was like a red rag to the bull instinct in Cowley. 'Why wasn't I informed?'

Abruptly, Dawson leaned forward. He dropped his smooth manner. He was hard and positive. 'Why wasn't I told about Doyle and Bodie?'

'I'm under no obligation to tell you anything.'

'That cuts both ways – '

'We've been weeks on this.' Cowley kept his fury down. 'Your interference could have jeopardised a very delicate operation.'

'That also cuts both ways.'

'I'm telling you, Dawson – '

'No. I'm telling you. Leave this office before one of us says something we'll both regret.'

For a moment, a long moment, the two men stared eyeball to eyeball. The moment hung, touch and go. Then Cowley straightened. 'You'll hear more of this.'

'I think we both will. I intend to inform the Minister.'

The head of CI5 stomped out to return to HQ, in as foul a mood as the infringement on his authority, he felt, gave him every right to be. He was muttering under his breath as he came in and Miss Walsh looked up over her spectacles.

'The arrogant, puffed up, conceited . . . '

'George – should I cover my ears?' She looked alertly at him as he calmed down a little. 'Someone's obviously ruffled your usual icy calm.'

'Yes. He goes by the name of Dawson.'

Elizabeth Walsh never forgot a name, and very little else for that matter. She gave a little bird-like nod as the memories clicked into place.

'Nigel Dawson. I knew him as a gangling youth with acne.'

'He's now acting head of MI6.'

'I *am* out of touch!'

Cowley humphed at that and put his glasses on. 'What have you got?'

'Two more, I'm afraid.' She gestured to the notice board where cards with scribbled notes had been pinned up and, more prominently, more disturbingly, two additional photographs. 'Wade and Moloney. Killed within the last three weeks.'

'Why wasn't it picked up?'

'They've both been retired for years. Why should anyone make the connection?'

That was true enough, and Cowley went on: 'Who were they?'

'Wade was a cypher clerk, Moloney worked in clerical records.'

Cowley took off his heavy glasses. 'It doesn't make sense. They were inactive. Why? Why kill these people?'

'The reason,' said Miss Walsh, 'is undoubtedly the key.'

'Work the puzzle board, Elizabeth.'

'I may need more pieces.'

'I'll do what I can. I have to go.'

As Cowley, with a smile, hurried off in his limping way, Miss Walsh went back to work. She wrote a name on one of the cards and then paused. She frowned. After a moment, slowly, she wrote a name on another card. She pinned the cards up on the puzzle board, parts of the picture that would unriddle the murders and attempted murder of little people.

Two names on the cards: NIGEL DAWSON. GEORGE COWLEY.

Bodie and Doyle in the computer room of CI5 HQ stared up at the puzzle board. Miss Walsh was not in the room, and the computer operators merely stared covertly at the two agents who were out in the field risking their necks.

Doyle jerked his head at the puzzle board. 'What's that supposed to be?'

'I don't know.' Bodie felt frisky. 'But I'll have a pound each way.'

Cowley limped in looking like Zeus ready to hurl a thunderbolt. He had had his interview with the Minister and Dawson had put the boot in and the Minister had decided that CI5 and MI6 must work together on this one. Cowley had his own ideas where his responsibilities lay.

'Bodie,' he snapped, crisply, admitting of no argument. 'You work with Williams. But you report to me, both of you. Nothing gets back to MI6. Clear?'

Bodie nodded. 'Right.'

Cowley looked fierce. 'I want the man behind this and I want him soon.'

Invisible behind his barrier of floodlights the man with the mid-European accent told Ferris exactly what he wanted done. Ferris licked his lips. He'd once been told by his probation officer that a deprived childhood did not necessarily give anyone the right to kill someone else.

'I think it's risky,' Ferris said.

'You're not paid to think.'

'But what's the rush? I mean – '

'Are you saying you can't do it?' The menace was unmistakable.

'No, no.' Ferris wished he had a sweet to suck. 'No. It's just the time.'

'If you think time is short, you must leave at once and get to work.' Ferris acknowledged the order and turned to leave, and the man added: 'Haven't you forgotten something?'

'Oh, yeah. The money.'

A bright glitteringly silver object flew up from the shadows, into the lights. It hit the floor and Ferris looked down.

It was a door key.

'Room twenty-eight.'

Ferris picked the key up. It was still warm from contact with the fingers of the invisible man lost beyond the flood of light.

'Thanks

The motel offered discreet service. Ferris opened the door of room twenty-eight without bother and went in. On the bed rested a case. Ferris smiled. Quite automatically he'd popped a chocolate into his mouth. He sucked with pleasure, opening the case, looking at the ranked piles of notes. The money was good, you had to say that about the man, funny accent and all.

Then Ferris's mouth fell open in surprise.

Lined up on the floor beside the bed were canvas holdalls. They were all the same, and each one was just like the ones he'd given out with instructions and money to his recruited hit-men. He shut his mouth. He counted.

Fourteen.

He knew what they were.

'Oh, my God,' said Ferris. He felt weak.

Fourteen – no wonder the man had been on about the time element.

He popped another chocolate into his mouth and felt better after that. He called Twig in and between them they carried the holdalls to their car. Twig did all this with a smooth and casual indifference. Ferris, sweets or no sweets, was in a highly agitated state. He kept fidgeting, and running his finger around inside his collar.

'What did he say?' Twig demanded once they'd stashed the bags in the back of the car.

'He said there'd been a change of plan.' Ferris sweated. 'It's been brought forward. We do the whole thing tomorrow.'

Twig jerked his head back. 'What. That lot?'

'That's what he wants.'

Twig ruminated. Then: 'We haven't got enough men.'

'Shut up – '

'What about back up?'

'Shut up, will you! I'm trying to think.'

Twig drew into himself, driving the car carefully, most desirous of not being stopped by an officious jumped-up bit of filth in his panda car.

'We'll work it out,' Ferris said. He felt a bit better. He started to unwrap a fresh bar of chocolate. 'We kill them all tomorrow.'

Dawn rose in a sullen mood. Blood-red light coated the flaccid waters of the river. The smells were thick and no early morning breeze blew fresh air in to wipe away the miasmas of the night. The air hung heavy. Somewhere a crane chug-chugged to itself. The ever-present rumble of distant traffic trembled almost inaudibly. The clothing factory looked as though it would fall down if someone opened the front door and took away its sole means of support.

Bodie eyed the place with the cold and professional eye of a man who was putting his head into a noose. Williams crouched beside him by the wall. Just as the MI6 man was about to step forward, Bodie grabbed his arm and hauled him back.

Silently, both men watched as the door opened.

The fellow who came out, walking smartly, his head a little bent as though he walked into an invisible breeze, carried a holdall.

The holdall was of a familiar shape to the agents.

Williams whispered. 'Do we take him?'

'No. Let him go.'

'You know what's in that bag. A photograph and an address. Someone's death warrant.'

Bodie hesitated. Of course Williams was right. But Bodie remembered Williams sitting in the car and letting a man get out and take a gun up a garden path and into a bungalow to murder an old lady. Williams had just sat and allowed that to happen. He was squeamish all of a sudden. Bodie had his orders, and was more confident that Cowley could handle that end than Williams could this.

'Let me call in,' said Williams.

'No.'

When the coast was clear they stood up, dusted off their trousers, and went into the clothing factory. It still smelled of dust and ancient chalk and mice. Twig was taking the last of the fourteen holdalls.

'One to go,' Twig said, quite unconcerned at the enormity of these proceedings.

'That's yours, Twig.' Ferris saw Bodie and Williams walking up between the racked clothes. 'Well, well. It's Mr Careful and nervous friend. What kept you?'

Bodie wrinkled that expressive Bodie lip. He glanced at his watch.

'We're early!'

Ferris laughed and draped a too-familiar arm over Bodie's shoulder. Bodie remained still.

'I'm kidding!' declared Ferris, expansively. 'I like you, both of you. That's why I'm giving you something special. It's worth twenty-five thousand each.'

The sum remained a meaningless amount in this deadly context.

Bodie said: 'For what?'

Ferris took his arm away from Bodie's elegantly clad shoulders and started to reach into his pocket. Bodie just watched. If Ferris thought . . .

'Maybe for sitting in a room.'

Ferris took his hand from his pocket and tossed across a key with an attached label.

'The address is on the tab.'

Williams, nervous, said: 'What's this all about?'

Ferris now produced a coconut-choccy bar and started to strip the paper. Bodie pointed an accusing finger at Williams as Ferris smiled his fat smile.

'Silly,' said Bodie, 'question.'

When they went off to their assignment, Bodie let Williams drive. The day was still overcast; but the skies showed signs of clearing up.

Bodie checked the address label on the key. The people

handling this were very careful. All this runaround clearly indicated that they were professionals, just like the Professionals.

'The address is Flat eight, Macefield House.' Bodie looked ahead through the screen. 'Stop at the next phone box.'

When Bodie rang the news through to Cowley, he received the obvious orders to carry on.

Macefield House turned out to be shabby, with red brick more brown than red, and concrete cracked and yellowed. As he had noticed this tiny touch before, Bodie noticed that just over fifty per cent of the dustbins in their bricked area still had lids. A good sign, that. Flat eight was empty, barren and dusty. No curtains, no carpets, an empty tea chest with a splintered hole in one side, and a telephone on the window sill. Beside the telephone a brown manila envelope struck a familiar touch.

Bodie ripped the manila open.

The money looked just like money.

'They never stop giving us money,' said Bodie. He shook his head.

The phone rang.

Williams looked at it, shocked that a phone should ring in a deserted flat.

Bodie scooped the receiver.

'Yeah?'

Ferris's fat voice said: 'Made yourself comfortable?'

'It,' said Bodie with considerable patience, 'is not exactly a suite at the Dorchester.'

'All right.' Ferris's voice brisked up. 'Now listen. You're the back-up. I'm relying on you.'

'Back-up for what?'

'Look outside. See if the milkman's been yet.'

The line went dead.

Williams started to frame a question. Bodie just opened the door and went outside. The day still smelled as though it should never have been woken up. He saw a single milk bottle, clean and polished, shiny, on the step. A sheet of paper was rolled up and stuck in the neck of the bottle.

Bodie just reached down and tweaked the paper out.

He did not think the milk bottle was a Molotov cocktail. This flat had been organised by people who knew what they were doing. He went back inside.

'What is it?' demanded Williams, all agog.

Bodie tucked his chin in as he read. He looked sick.

'A list. Names and addresses.'

When Cowley looked down the list handed to him by Bodie in the CI5 HQ Computer Room, he, like his agents, had no need to be told what it was. But he was human – although Bodie and Doyle wouldn't take bets on it – and he could not refrain from exclaiming: 'My God. It's a death list.'

Bodie and Williams stood stoney faced as Cowley read on.

'You two were to cover anyone who missed.'

Doyle fidgeted and then said: 'How many?'

Cowley showed his concern.

'Fourteen.'

At this Miss Walsh looked up from her desk. Her face reflected the concern they all felt. Fourteen innocent people were to be gunned down unless Cowley and his people of CI5 could prevent the mass murders.

'I want every available man briefed.' Cowley gave his orders in a firm sharp voice. 'And get me copies of this fast.'

The operator took the list away for repro. Cowley took his glasses off. His face looked like a walnut with the strain they all felt. Williams stepped forward.

'Fourteen targets. It's too many for you to handle. Call in MI6.'

'No,' Cowley told the MI6 agent. 'CI5 handles it.'

'I'm going to call Dawson . . . '

Williams started for the nearest phone.

Cowley caught Doyle's eye as Williams passed near him.

Cowley nodded.

Doyle took Williams by the arm and swung him round.

The MI6 agent did not misunderstand what these people of CI5 intended. He looked enraged.

'You're making a mistake, Cowley.'

Cowley simply ignored Williams, spoke to Bodie and Doyle.

'Take him out.'

The partners escorted Williams away.

Miss Walsh, who had been quietly working away at her desk, looked up as George Cowley limped over to her. She could see the strain on him, the lines deeply indented in his face. She remembered when he'd been a dashingly handsome agent, even though he'd always limped as far as she knew, and he was still handsome in his square open way, with the sandy hair glinting. He did look oppressed, though, by the decisions he had made.

The puzzle board now bore a freight of colour: pins, cards, string. The photographs would now dramatically multiply.

Cowley looked up at the puzzle board.

'Red for times and dates. Blue for personal contact. Green for . . . '

'Green for letters and phone calls.'

'Ah, yes. I'd forgotten.'

He pulled his spectacles off, heavy authoritative glasses, and tapped them on his open palm.

'You were right to keep it internal,' said Miss Walsh. She paused. Then: 'Can CI5 cope?'

Cowley said: 'I hope so.'

CI5 moved into action.

The Squad, the Big A, were out to prevent mass murder.

Well, it made a nice change.

It so happened that the address Bodie handled first was the one to which the man he and Williams had seen leaving the clothing factory had been assigned.

Had the assassin failed, then Bodie and Williams in the deserted flat in Macefield would have been alerted to go and do the job properly. As it was – here came the fellow carrying his holdall, walking as bold as brass up the path between the shrubbery.

The area was quiet, residential, the most noise coming from kids playing and the Ding-Dong Man in his ice-cream van. Why anyone living here should be the target for murder remained a puzzle.

The fellow carrying his holdall reached the bush where Bodie waited for him. Bodie stepped out to the man's rear and simply pushed his revolver up into the side of the neck, under the ear, most painfully.

'One move,' said Bodie in his silky voice. 'One move and you lose the back of your skull, chum.'

He reached in under the would-be assassin's coat and took out the Walther PPK. This he placed in his own coat pocket. Then he bundled the man out through the front garden onto the pavement. The man looked bewildered. He still clutched his holdall as though it was a lifebelt.

The CI5 car parked just far enough away from the house not to arouse suspicion tooled up with Pocock at the wheel.

Bodie leaned into the open window and scooped the R/T.

As he lifted the R/T handset he sensed that the fellow might think of making a run for it. Bodie half-turned. He looked exceedingly ferocious in a smooth, deadly way. He did not smile.

'Don't even think about it.'

The man slumped. He thought better of it.

Bodie called control. 'I've got him. Four is safe.'

That left the other thirteen.

The other thirteen were being dealt with as fast as CI5 operatives could get there and carry out their duties.

Ray Doyle caught number eight.

A TV rental van, as cover perfectly simple and efficient, drew up outside the target's house. Watching the street, Doyle saw the TV van and marked it down. When he saw the man getting out of the TV van carrying a holdall Doyle reacted.

The would-be assassin had to walk past Doyle's parked car to reach the front of the house. As he reached the car, Doyle flung the door open. The man, caught unprepared, staggered back.

Doyle whipped out of the car and confronted him.

There was always just the chance he *was* a TV man . . .

'What's in the bag?'

The fellow recovered. He did not answer.

Doyle spat out: 'I asked you a question.'

With a yell the man swung the bag at Doyle's head. It was quick and sudden and savage. Doyle ducked; but the sharp edge of the bag clipped Doyle on the side of the head and knocked him off balance.

Recovering, and cursing his own stupidity, Doyle sprinted after the fugitive who raced away and vanished around the next corner.

The corner led onto an alley, clean and used as a service road to the rear of the houses. There was no sign of the man, and then Doyle spotted him attempting to scale the high brick wall at the far end. A cat spat at them both; and ran back into his garden. Doyle started to run down the alley.

When he got near enough he slowed down and just ambled the last few yards.

The man was halfway over the wall; but he was hampered by the holdall and got himself caught halfway. His legs flailed the air as he tried to haul himself up and over to safety.

He was making a lot of grunting noise and heaving and humping, trying to get over.

Doyle drew his handgun from inside his coat and then, with a reflective gesture, rubbed the barrel down the side of his nose.

Ray Doyle wasn't sure if he should laugh or swear.

He looked up.

The two legs in brushed denim flailed away like a can-can dancer's legs.

'You wouldn't,' observed Doyle, 'want to be shot from

this angle, would you? Might alter your whole outlook on life.'

The can-can legs stilled. The man froze.

Roughly, Doyle said: 'Get down here.'

He reached up and yanked a leg. The man tumbled off the wall. He landed full of fight, leaping up and swinging the bag around again. He clearly thought he was still in with a chance. He was a beefy man, high-coloured, light on his feet despite his bulk.

Doyle did not mess with him.

The ex-policeman ducked the savagely-swung bag, dived in and tackled the fellow. He crashed him to the ground, not much caring which part of his anatomy he hit, grabbed or twisted, held him down with one hand, bearing down with full force.

The man tried to yell and Doyle thumped down.

The man stayed quiet.

A quick rummage through the holdall with his free hand confirmed to Doyle that he had the right culprit. He stood up and put a foot into the small of the would-be murderer's back. He stood on that foot for a moment, just to let the guy know the situation, and then turned the photograph from the holdall over.

He pulled out his R/T.

'This is 4.5. Wilson's clear.'

Control came back with fresh instructions . . .

In the computer room as the reports came in Cowley ticked off the numbers on the list.

'Wilson,' he said. 'Number eight. That leaves just one.'

As he looked up, worried, Miss Walsh gave him a small smile of encouragement. The last one would be reached quickest either by Bodie or Doyle, they were both within striking distance.

Thirteen would-be murderers had been accounted for, and the agents of CI5 had worked fast. Anderson and Hailsham brought their catches in, to be followed by Pocock, who had left Bodie to tackle the last one, and Rogers. Thirteen down, one to go . . .

Cowley took his glasses off and tapped them on his palm. He returned Miss Walsh's smile; but until that last one had been accounted for he would not rest easy. And, even then, he'd not rest easy until he knew who was ordering these people to be murdered. . .

Bodie and Doyle in their own cars hurtled towards the nearest street that would give access to the boatyard. Boatyards, besides being on the banks of rivers, generally tended to be places not too easy of access. Just why this fact of life should be so escaped the agents.

The street that was the nearest point lay quiet and dozing. The air was nice and fresh and the overcast was beginning to drift away. A few hesitant splotches of sunshine appeared and disappeared.

Bodie's car hurtled along the street, flat out, the noise of its engine disturbing the tranquillity.

Doyle's car hurtled along the street, flat out, its engine doing just what Bodie's car's engine was doing.

They roared towards each other, the race to be first a drawn contest. The two cars braked fiercely, screeching, skidding on burning rubber as they slewed to a halt facing each other.

Bodie and Doyle hopped out.

Their prisoners, one in each car, sat back, shivering at the maniacs who had captured them.

The partners walked to the bonnets of their cars and looked at the gap between.

With the ex-policeman's air of giving factual evidence at the scene of an accident, Doyle said:

'Three inches.'

With his infuriating air of brash optimism, cheerfully, Bodie gauged it and said:

'Four inches.'

Doyle looked heavenwards, for Bodie could be so Bodie-ish at times it was painful, and said: 'I see we've both got passengers.'

'Yeah. Take care of them. I'll check the house.'

Bodie vaulted over the gate and headed for the front of

the house. Everything seemed very quiet after the racket of the arrival of the two cars.

'All right,' said Doyle to the prisoners. 'You two – out!'

They emerged, badly shaken, thankful still to be each in one piece. Brisklv, Doyle handcuffed them together. A woman answered the door to Bodie and they talked as Doyle clicked the cuffs. Bodie sprinted back down the path.

'He's down at his boat. Fuller's Yard.'

He ran across to his car.

As he ran he tossed his partner his handcuffs.

'Here.'

Bodie's car started at the turn of the key.

Working rapidly, Doyle hauled the two men to the nearest lamp post. He was not particularly gentle with them. He slapped Bodie's cuffs on the wrist of the fellow he had taken off the wall, passed them around the lamp post and clicked the other cuff onto Bodie's prisoner. The two were chained up to the post.

Bodie reversed his car and hauled it around Doyle's with a protesting squeal of rubber tyres.

The men at the foot of the lamp post looked. There was no way they were going to break free.

Doyle said: 'Don't go away,' and raced for Bodie's car.

The car was already moving, the passenger door swinging open. Doyle leaped, grabbed, got a grip and hauled himself inside. He slammed the door. He puffed his lips out.

'Whew!'

The car roared off.

The boatyard pushed a bright splash of multi-coloured interest into the grey morning. Sunshine fitfully touched the hulls of the boats and gleamed off copper and brass. The water lapped gently. Mitchell's boat was drawn up so that he could get at her properly. The robust smells of tar and paint and oil mingled and drowned the smell of mud. There were very few people about yet; Mitchell had his gangway to himself, lovingly painting the hull of *Eliza Jane*, a sweet little craft.

Mitchell himself was white-haired and ruddy-faced, a stout man in his late fifties. He applied the red paint carefully.

A footfall on the wooden treads caught his attention and he turned, looking up.

The man approaching looked completely out of place in his natty gent's city suiting.

Mitchell wore an old sweater and pants that were liberally smeared with paint.

The man walked up, smoothly, not hurrying. He stopped.

'Looking for a Mr Mitchell.'

'You've found him.' Mitchell still held the paint brush loaded with red paint.

At this reply, Twig moved forward, and he was alert and dangerous. This was his trade, he was good at it, and he did not make mistakes.

'Mr H. R. Mitchell?'

'That's right.'

Twig put a hand inside his elegant jacket. Anyone looking on would imagine he was feeling for a letter.

'I've got – er – ' said Twig.

It was not a letter. Twig whipped out his Walther PPK and pointed it at Mitchell.

'Something for you,' said Twig.

The ruddy face blanched to match the hair as Mitchell stumbled back in horror. He kicked over the tin of paint.

Twig did not give his victim time to scream out.

Calmly, as though shooting in a .22 booth at a fair, Twig gunned Mitchell down.

Then, repocketing his pistol, he looked about and saw an anchor and chain a little further along. He hefted the anchor. Then he started to gather up the links.

The paint from the overturned tin spread in a pool, began to drip down over the ramp leading to the water's edge, a bright brilliant red.

Chapter Three

Bodie burned rubber belting the car through the narrow alleyway between the houses and out into the area with the boatyard at the far end. The uneven ground, pitted and roughly filled with broken bricks, jolted the car savagely.

The rows of boats drawn up out of the water, the general air of a place normally busy and now deserted, gave the partners the sense that time was running out.

Bodie slammed the brakes on and the car slewed and skidded over the loose ground, screeched to a halt.

The CI5 agents leaped out, guns already in their fists, started to run towards the boats, heading for *Eliza Jane*.

Doyle shouted as he spotted the upturned tin of paint and the redness spilling just beyond. He skidded to a halt and looked past the jumble of boat fittings.

A body lay on the ground wrapped in chains, an anchor weighing it all down. It was clear to Doyle that Twig had been interrupted by their arrival, had dropped the man wrapped in chains he was about to throw into the river. It had to be Twig. He was the only one, apart from Ferris and whoever was behind it all, they hadn't rounded up.

'Bodie!' bellowed Doyle.

His partner had gone racing off around the other way.

Among the on-shore boats, Bodie heard his partner's yell.

'What?' He shouted back.

'He's close.'

Twig heard them shouting.

He moved cautiously alongside the hull of a boat, gun at the ready, peered around the stern. The rudder had been removed and he peered out between the fittings. He couldn't see anyone. He started to edge out, intending to make a break back to the road and his car.

Suddenly Twig spotted Bodie at the far side of a small cabin cruiser.

Instantly, Twig lifted the Walther PPK and triggered a shot.

The slug slapped past Bodie and struck the ground beyond.

Bodie disappeared from view.

Twig turned the other way, retreating, trying to get back to the road.

Up on top of the boats, jumping recklessly from deck to deck, Ray Doyle headed for the sound of the shot.

He almost missed his footing and went headfirst through a skylight. He recovered, cursed himself for a tangle-footed oaf, and jumped cleanly onto the deck of the next boat.

Bodie yelled out again.

'Can you see him?'

'No!' hollered Doyle, leaping from deck to deck.

Twisting around, keeping down, Bodie peered between the hulls of the boats. He caught a quick fleeting glimpse of Twig breaking past the open space between the boats at the end and he let rip two quick shots. He knew he hadn't hit the bastard, but he'd gee'd him up, all right.

Twig ran on and then spun about, as a crashing sound at his back brought him up all standing. One of Bodie's shots had knocked a tin can off a deck. It crashed and clanged away and long before Twig had recognised what it was, he'd fired a desperate spray of bullets.

The CI5 agents heard that sound.

They closed in, one running along an alley between the boats, the other leaping down and belting along the next alley. They broke out at the far end, looked about, guns at the ready. There was no sign of Twig.

Bodie looked along the riverline, among the boats.

Doyle started there and looked up towards the bank and the road. The backs of the houses cut off the farther view.

'There he is!' exclaimed Doyle.

Twig was desperately clambering up the muddy bank,

sliding and slipping, making for the road. The ground was broken and tufty, with a few ancient and rotting boats lying around. Doyle lifted his handgun.

It was a tricky shot. Doyle steadied himself. He'd once been the champion pistol shot in the Met. He fired.

The distant figure of Twig, scrabbling up in a frenzy of despair to escape, suddenly stopped scrambling up.

That nattily-suited figure swayed.

The arms flew out, the head lolled. The figure collapsed and fell.

Twig fell headlong down the bank to crash into the bottom of an abandoned boat. He sprawled there, his gun tumbled from his fist.

Doyle said: 'He wasn't born lucky.'

The partners started off to clear up the mess and see about Mr H. R. Mitchell.

Mr H. R. Mitchell's photograph was now pinned up on Miss Walsh's puzzle board along with all the others.

The board was now a mass of photos, cards and coloured lines, like a superior Jackson Pollock, and Miss Walsh stood looking at it with Cowley. Both their faces reflected the gravity of the situation.

'You shouldn't blame yourself,' Elizabeth Walsh told Cowley. 'All the others are safe.'

'Who else should I blame?'

She wouldn't allow him to continue like that. She turned his attention back to the business in hand and the puzzle board.

'Something's beginning to emerge; but it's a negative.'

'Go on.'

'Fifteen men and three women, all working at some time for Intelligence. But they were record and cypher clerks, low level couriers, typists – small fry.'

'So why did someone want them dead?'

'Because,' suggested Miss Walsh, 'of something they possessed.'

Cowley nodded. 'Information.'

'It has to be. But that's the negative. They never had access to top secrets. They seem to know nothing of importance.'

Cowley considered This was all very interesting, but it had to lead somewhere.

'Individually they know nothing of significance. But suppose each holds the tiny piece of a jig-saw.'

Miss Walsh was well up with Cowley, if not ahead of him.

'Collectively,' she said, 'they can complete the picture.'

'The picture of the man who wanted them dead.'

They brooded on the puzzle board and its freight of significant colour. It was trying to tell them something; they had to understand how to read what it was telling them.

Miss Walsh picked up a pen, ready to start work again. Then, with a bird-like motion of her head she looked at Cowley.

'Where are they now?'

'We've got them under protection. They're safe.'

'I think,' said Miss Walsh in her finest manner, 'I really think we should go and talk to them.'

Bodie and Doyle kept an observation on the clothing factory, scene of one or two fraught incidents in their incident-packed lives, from a battered old mini van. The van was small but there was enough leg room to stretch out. The factory looked more deserted than usual, even the sun gave it the go by, and the building lay in shadow.

Doyle was keeping this watch through the rear windows, and Bodie was stretched out, taking it easy.

For a man who had roughed it as a mercenary in Africa, Bodie tended to like his creature comforts. He wore a lazy smile as he stretched out, and Doyle crouched by the window.

Bodie put his hands behind his head, and uncrossed and crossed his legs, squirming to get more comfortable on the old mattress they'd bunged in the back of the van.

'We're wasting our time,' he said. 'He'd be a fool to come back here.'

Doyle spotted movement past the end of the building; but he said nothing as his partner chattered on. Ferris appeared in view of Doyle through the van window, creeping along cautiously towards the sliding doors. He carried a can. It was a petrol can; but that didn't mean it carried petrol now.

Bodie said, again, with satisfaction: 'He'd be a fool to come back here.'

'Crazy,' agreed Doyle.

'Although,' went on Bodie, 'he wasn't the brightest thing on two legs.'

Watching the subject of the conversation as he reached the doors and slid one back, Doyle said: 'I thought he was sweet.'

'What?'

'All those sweets he eats.'

Doyle watched Ferris go into the clothing factory. Then he looked down at the recumbent form of Bodie. He spoke perfectly dead pan.

'He just went in the door.'

You wouldn't get Bodie going like that. He answered in just as dead pan a voice as Doyle's: 'I was right. He's an idiot.'

They climbed out of the van and padded off towards the clothing factory and the shut sliding doors.

Inside Ferris twisted the cap off the can. His face looked dazed, sheened in sweat, more than nervous. He began spraying the contents of the can over everything he could reach.

The raw stink of petrol fumes filled the air.

A bang crashed against the door.

Ferris jumped and dropped the can.

Doyle's voice hammered through the door.

'We know you're in there.'

The Walther PPK appeared in Ferris's fist as he faced the door. He'd drawn it fast enough. His lips trembled.

Doyle's voice blasted again.

'Come out. Hands over your head.'

With a scuttling movement like a drunken crab trying and failing to run sideways, Ferris ran to the door He put his ear to the wood, trying to listen.

He could hear nothing except the hammering of his heart.

Outside that shut door Bodie gave a circling motion to his hand, and Doyle nodded. Bodie would angle around the back.

When Bodie vanished around the corner of the building, Doyle very very carefully leaned from one side of the door out towards the centre.

He gave a hefty fist thump on the wood. Then he drew back immediately.

A splatter of shots hissed and cracked through the panel.

Ferris, trembling held the gun at the ready. When that infuriating, menacing thump sounded on the door again he triggered the Walther. He pumped shot after shot through the door.

And then the gun clicked empty.

He just threw it aside and ran back towards the petrol soaked area. His foot kicked the empty can.

A tremendous crash of broken glass snapped him around.

He stared up, sickly, as Bodie appeared in the office window, draped in broken window frame, scattering shards of glass everywhere. Bodie appeared like the Angel of the Lord, ready to strike down evil doers.

'End of the line, fat man,' said Bodie.

Ferris licked his lips. He was cornered. And he was desperate.

He hauled out a box of matches. His fumbling fingers spilled the white sticks until he got one to hold. He held the head against the side of the box. His eyes were mad.

Ferris snarled up at Bodie: 'The place is soaked in petrol. I've got matches here.'

Bodie could smell the stink of petrol fumes.

He looked down on Ferris. Bodie's face, smooth and hard, expressed great concern.

'Go ahead,' said Bodie. 'Go on, strike it. You're the one who'll fry.'

The moment of tension stretched.

In that petrol-soaked area with the clothing ready to burst into flame like so many bombs, Ferris would surely fry. But the flames would leap up and engulf Bodie, too. Perhaps Ferris was enough of a fanatic to strike the match . . .

The look on Ferris's face told the story.

He dropped the matches. He just let them go any old where. He was shaking; but he was not shaking so much that he could not reach into his pocket.

Bodie's gun did not waver.

The fat man produced a piece of chocolate and started stripping the paper and foil away.

Then Bodie relaxed.

The men and women so rapidly snatched, as one of the dazed people put it, 'from the Jaws of Death', were brought by the rear entrance into the scruffy interior of CI5 HQ. A dusty store room was rapidly emptied of boxes and racks and a few beds brought in. Food was sent in, remarkably good food from a Bakeaway around the corner. CI5 interior guards stood around, unobtrusively, but always on the alert.

One by one the survivors, as survivors they were indeed, were ushered into a small interview room alongside the computer centre. George Cowley and Miss Elizabeth Walsh conducted the interviews.

Charles Lewis, silver-haired and in his early sixties, neatly-dressed, established that he had worked in central records for almost two years, until he retired, in October of 1975.

'I think that's about it,' said Cowley. 'Thank you for your co-operation.'

As Lewis left the room Miss Walsh asked him to send in

the next one, Mr Harold Flynn.

Lewis left and Cowley said: 'How many more?'

'Two, after Flynn.'

'You worked with Flynn, didn't you?'

She nodded. 'For a few months. I think you'll find him forthright.'

As the door opened and the guard ushered in Flynn, Cowley was thinking that a spot of forthrightness was needed right now. He seemed to be getting absolutely nowhere in this maze. They were dredging through the dusty memories of retired folk, seeking the clues to modern murder. Flynn was a well-preserved man of about fifty, dressed in a sweater, jacket and slacks. He looked pretty fit.

He smiled as he walked in.

'Miss Walsh! It's been a long time.'

'Twelve years.' She indicated the Chief of CI5 at her side. 'This is George Cowley, head of CI5.'

'Mr Cowley.'

Cowley asked Flynn to sit down and then said: 'Tell me, have you any idea why someone would want to kill you?'

Flynn crossed his legs, sitting back. 'I might have.'

Cowley gave Miss Walsh a look which summed up both their feelings.

'For eight years,' said Flynn, 'I worked in the box at Orly.'

'The decoding centre.'

'Yes, I was senior British cypher clerk.'

'Attached to the army,' Miss Walsh added.

'Correct. But I was still officially MI5.'

'What exactly were your duties?' said Cowley.

'We handled top level despatches, documents, orders for NATO. The stuff was being flown in all the time. One day a coded batch of letters went missing.'

'Important?' Miss Walsh leaned forward.

'Very. The balloon went up. They got them back.'

'Yes.' Cowley recalled. 'The Russian courier was caught trying to get to the coast. I remember the panic.'

'The point is, with the security set up at Orly, it had to be an inside job. And someone near the top.'

'I don't know his name. I don't even know what he looks like.'

Cowley and Doyle, stone-faced as Easter Island statues just stared at Ferris.

His voice shook. He was pleading. 'Please.'

Cowley stood up. He stalked across to Ferris. He leaned down and put his face close to the sweaty mask. 'I'm going to give you one chance.'

Ferris agreed to co-operate completely. Cowley ran him out to the Green Dragon Motel whilst Bodie and Doyle followed in their car.

'Don't try anything stupid,' Cowley advised Ferris as Ferris alighted. 'We'll hear every word.'

The miniature transmitter, the size of a button, was dropped into Ferris's top pocket. He swallowed and sweated and then went into the motel. Bodie turned on the tape recorder in the car and they all listened to Ferris walking along the corridor.

Ferris knocked on the door, was told to wait, and then to enter. He braced himself. Then he went in. The flood of light bathed him in brilliance. He stood, lumpily.

The voice with the mid-European accent, the voice Doyle had dubbed the Brown Bear voice, said: 'Why did you ask for this meeting?'

'I want to get out of the country.'

'Buy your way out. You were paid enough.'

Listening to all this, Cowley spoke into his R/T to his agents.

'Let's take him.'

Ferris still spoke on, shaking. 'I need papers – a passport –'

'Why should I give you papers?'

'I could be useful. I could work for you in another country.'

'You are a fool.'

The sound of running feet reached Ferris from the corridor like the sound of angels' wings. He braced himself up.

'No. You're the fool!'

The door burst open and Cowley and two CI5 men belted in, guns drawn. They reacted to the lights, and then the mid-European voice said with loaded sarcasm: 'Do you really think I would walk into a trap?'

Cowley leaped forward and smashed aside the array of lights. They spilled over, spraying brilliance everywhere like an encapsulated fireworks display. Beyond the lights stood a table and electronic apparatus. Cowley felt the anger in him – tricked! The man hadn't been here at all, only the loudspeaker to transmit his voice. He dashed across to the window and looked out. A black foreign car was just pulling away.

Cowley ripped his R/T free and snarled into it.

'The car on the slip road. A black saloon –'

Bodie and Doyle in their motor reacted at once and Doyle gunned the car away and towards the car park at the rear from whence they could reach the slip road.

They spotted the black saloon immediately and Doyle spun the wheel. The foreign car howled past the exit and up the ramp, and Doyle, following, found another car pulling into the way. Without hesitation the ex-copper punched the car clean through the entrance, mounting the kerb and splintering the red and white barrier into smithereens. Tyres screeching, the cars pelted up for the main road.

Traffic was oddly light on this side of the road. The fugitive had a clear run. He turned in his seat to look back. The pursuing car had been joined by another; but he was confident his car had the legs of them. He swung back to look ahead and his face contorted in horror.

One side of the road was dug up and masses of yellow and black earth spilled pyramids festooned with barriers and lamps. The traffic lights stood at red. Now oncoming traffic could drive through the single lane, and a large van blocked the whole width.

The man who had hired murderers stamped his foot onto the brake, slewing the car wildly. He skidded broadside on into a pile of sand. He was shaken but unhurt, and words obscene. ' "A sad loss .. a valued servant." The man was a spy, a Russian agent '

'No point in washing one's dirty linen in public, Cowley.'

With the air of a man rejecting everything, not caring over a small point in order to make a greater, Cowley said: 'Give the press what you like.'

He turned to go, crumpling the paper, leaving the billiards table and the opulence of the gentleman's club and the aroma of old-school-tie. Then, meaningfully, he turned to the Minister.

'What concerns me is how many more Dawsons there are.'

Chapter Four

Flags flew on public buildings for somebody-or-other's birthday, the sun was beginning to coax people into removing the top layers of clothing, sports fixtures burst the time schedules, the pubs were full and in the midst of all this outgoing happiness the hospital crouched at the centre like a spider in its web.

The forecourt of the hospital, as usual, bustled with activity. People trudged in and out, orderlies wheeled patients, nurses, chattering like parcels of cage-birds, tripped along, their neat capes like wings. Ambulances trilled their bells along the cross street fronting the hospital to swerve around the corner, and the other vehicles dutifully got out of the way.

There was a smell of spring in the air and the blossoms filled every nook and cranny with their perfumes. Against this glorious if brief fragrance even the stink from vehicle exhausts was for a time vanquished. And Mickey Hamilton stared at all this busy bustle searching for a doctor. Any doctor.

Hamilton concentrated on the forecourt of the hospital. He was a man in his early forties, with a lived-in face, and he was quite clearly under considerable mental stress. At one time, a few years ago, he'd dressed fashionably. Nowadays he didn't even remember to think about his appearance, and as a result he looked on the nondescript side of scruffy.

A group of nurses, laughing and enjoying the sunshine, trooped out of the hospital and down the steps. They waited at the kerb for a car to pass and then crossed, chattering, chattering. Hamilton peered through the telescopic sight at them, and then relaxed.

He spoke into his handset.

'Okay, we scored it right.'

Bodie was prowling. '*Who* did?' he said, fretfully.

'You can get the forensic boys up here,' went on Doyle.

'Doesn't make sense does it?'

'What, exactly?'

'Well,' said Bodie. 'What would you do? They've paid you some bread – '

Doyle nodded, interrupting. 'Dirty bills in a suitcase in Geneva airport.'

'Half down if you're lucky, half on delivery of a life-extinct ambassador. You gonna want that second suitcase?'

'I'm not going to miss like these jokers. I'm not going to go for a close hit – too much chance of identification, being picked up even. I'll back off. But not way up here, with so many down below.' Doyle's mop of curly hair moved, it seemed, of its own accord as he shook his head. 'No, it doesn't make sense.'

'So,' said Bodie, 'we scratch the pros.'

'Signs are there was only one of 'em.'

'Has to be a first time amateur, leaving all these traces. Trouble is – it just makes it all the harder to find him.'

'Or *stop* him, if he wants to try for this feller again.'

The partners looked one at the other. The puzzle filled their minds, but, despite that, suddenly, Doyle said:

'Hell!'

'What?'

'The girls . . .'

By the time they'd ridden back in the police car the girls were resigned to this situation. They were leaning on the bonnet of the Capri. Toni spoke reflectively.

'We try to see each other every other Tuesday. Sometimes every other Sunday. That means I see him on average once every three weeks.'

'How well do you know my one?' said Pat, falling into this almost familial relationship of hardship.

Toni threw her head back, smiling at memories. 'We double-dated a couple of months back. He tried to talk me away from Ray.' The memory evidently amused her as well as tickling her vanity. 'Oh, there they are –'

The police car pulled up and the two CI5 men jumped out.

Toni went on speaking, giving sage advice. 'No, don't get excited. Look at them. I can tell. It's "Goodbye girls. Give you a ring soon. Duty calls." If we're lucky we'll get a lift home in a squad car.' She sniffed, a beautiful girl feeling sorry for herself. 'The neighbours love it.'

Bodie and Doyle walked up like cats about to steal cream, smirks on their faces concealing their real feelings. Each took his girl by the arm, attempting to be nice and diplomatic.

'Sorry, luv,' said Bodie.

'Going to have to take another rain check,' said Doyle.

Bodie said: 'Want a ride back? We'll ask the sergeant to give you a lift . . .'

The voices of the partners trailed off at the girls' icy stares and general air of wishing that two certain flamboyant gentlemen might drop dead.

Mickey Hamilton took the bus back to the block of council flats he now called home. The lift was working. This was not a small miracle; it was a major miracle. He alighted at the top floor and let himself into his flat. He went through the lounge into the kitchen, and then back again, and slumped down in the sofa. The place was a shambles, with dirty crockery piled up, newspapers lying about, the revolting remains of half-eaten meals, half-drunk cups of tea and coffee, piles of dirty clothing waiting to be laundered. He found an overturned glass on the floor by the sofa and then lurched across to the sideboard and found the scotch. He was shaking. He poured and gulped the spirit down.

He wandered across to the window, opened it and looked out.

Someone rang the bell; but he ignored that small distraction. He remained sunk in his misery. Eventually the caller yanked up the key on its string through the letter box and let herself in. It was his sister Kay. Mrs Costa was a little older than her brother, a neat, respectable woman, and she was horrified at the state of the place.

She berated him in a sisterly way for letting himself go.

'Want a bit of shopping done, don't you? A bit of cleaning –'

'No, Kay, I'm managing. You don't have to bother. Best thing is to stay away from me, let me get on with things.'

'This is managing, is it? Look at it all. You enjoy giving me all this extra work, don't you?'

She started to bustle about making an attempt at tidying up.

'Nobody asks you to come up here, practically force your way in –'

His sister looked up, flushed. 'You know what they're saying? "Mrs Costa, he needs to be looked after. Do you think you can cope?" That's what they said. That's what I'm doing. I'm trying to cope with you and all your crazy moods. I'm doing my best, Mick.' She pushed a strand of hair from her forehead. 'And not a word of thanks from you. If it wasn't for me, they wouldn't have let you come home, would they?'

As she glared at him he mutely shook his head.

'Do you want to go back there?' She was fierce, now. 'Is that what you want? More doctors? Course you don't.'

'No. Listen, Kay.' His face looked crumpled. 'I was over at the the flats –'

She interrupted, not wanting to hear about the old flats they were pulling down.

'Mick, that's all past. Those days are gone. You've got to live in the present, think about the future.'

'That's what I'm doing. Maybe I can stop these things happening again. But is it right?'

She took some comfort from what he said, even if he did look dreadful.

'Course it is, if you try, do your best.'

Hamilton felt the desire to confide in his sister, to tell her what he had done, almost overwhelm him.

'I don't think you understand –' he began

'Oh no? Well, I understand you have to eat So I'm going down the shops. Stock you up. Then I'll come back, do some tidying. And you shouldn't be on your own brooding, should you?'

'Kay.' Hamilton spoke with a desperation his sister, bustling around ready to leave, completely missed. 'Listen –'

'*You* listen. You'll come and eat with us tonight, and we'll think about what to do next.'

He followed her as she walked with her determined swing into the hall. He looked unfocused, in despair, clutching at will-o'-the-wisps and finding them of no help.

'Perhaps,' she said as she opened the door, 'you should move in with Vic and me again. Like you did after – you know – after what happened to Maureen.'

The mention of the name Maureen visibly affected Hamilton. But Kay went out the door, brisk about her business for her brother. He slammed the door. He was shaking again. Viciously, he yanked the key off the string and hurled it somewhere into the depths of the flat. He headed into the lounge again and made for the scotch.

The street sounds from the open window drew him like a magnet. Glass in hand he walked across. The noises spurted up, motor car engines, squeals from tyres, the hum and tramp of people. And then, hideously mingled with these ordinary noises, he heard moans, cries of pain, a distorted cacophony of suffering.

He couldn't stand it.

Nothing he could do would help blot out those awful sounds.

Trembling, he clutched the whisky glass.

Then, in a vain and empty gesture to drive back the phantom sounds, a despairing defence against fate, he hurled the glass through the window.

On the street below the glass fell to shatter into whirring splinters close by a middle-aged lady wheeling a shopping basket on wheels. She jumped and looked around, at first scared, then confused, and then angry.

Hamilton's sister Kay passed by at that moment and heard the crash.

The middle-aged lady looked upset and angry.

'Terrible, isn't it,' said Kay sympathetically. 'They ought to be locked up.'

Bodie and Doyle carried out investigations in the areas each knew best. As an ex-para, ex-mercenary, ex a whole lot of unholy things, Bodie's contacts were wide and unconventional. As an ex-detective constable, Doyle's contacts were of the more conventional kind but none-theless exotic for that.

Doyle ambled along the pavement where gaudy neon signs painted the stone with a multicoloured wonderland. Canned music bleated on the night air. There was a lot of activity and some laughter as he neared the night club that was his goal. It was seedy. It had a certain unsavoury reputation.

Iron steps led down to the basement entrance. From that pit of radiance mellower reggae music floated up.

A very large, very aggressive, very hard black man leaned against the railings, smoking a cigarette. As Doyle ambled up the black man blew a plume of smoke in Doyle's general direction.

The ex-copper sniffed, smiled, ambled on.

The big black bouncer looked down into the area and called down.

'Mr Lemon.'

A moment or two later, as Doyle stopped and waited, Mr Lemon climbed the iron steps.

He was dressed as an expensive accountant might dress, smart grey suit, polished shoes, nice tie. But, on his fingers, extravagant rings, blazing with jewellery, proclaimed that Mr Lemon was no accountant – at least, not of the common or garden variety . . .

He saw Doyle.

'Don't want no trouble, Mr Doyle. There's a good feller.'

Doyle looked cool.

'Don't think I want any either.' He eyed the big black bouncer 'I want Sylvester.'

Mr Lemon looked outraged. 'Why would *I* know where he is? Ain't seen him today. Don't see him every day.'

'This is the day he collects his – what d'you call it these days? Insurance?'

Mr Lemon's lips compressed. Then he said: 'Public relations.'

Doyle smiled, the lump under his right eye most pronounced in the lurid neon lighting.

'Well, when he does show, tell him I'll be very angry if he doesn't come hunt me up.'

Mr Lemon was now clearly a very worried man.

'What's it about?'

Doyle wanted to defuse the pyrotechnic implications bursting away in Mr Lemon's head.

'He just may know something *I* need to know. Nobody has to get hassled. Unless he doesn't come see me.'

'But s'pose he doesn't show *here*?'

Doyle's face grew grim. 'Then you go look for him. Or I might have to get naughty – all around.'

He poked the bouncer in the chest with a stiff forefinger, sniffed the air again and with meaning, and then ambled off.

Mr Lemon looked after him, turned on the bouncer and ripped the cigarette from his mouth.

He threw it away, hunched his shoulders, and went back down the iron steps.

The management called the place a hotel. It took in paying guests; apart from that calling it a hotel demanded the attentions of inspectors checking up on the Trades Descriptions Act.

There was dust in the air and damp underfoot. The residents mouldered away in the lounge as the lounge itself mouldered away. In the corner at a table for two sat Frank Armstrong, still in his forties, but in the ravaged forties, a tough hulk of a man reduced to a husk. He drank from his own bottle of scotch. He did nothing by his drinking to alleviate the shakes. His clothes bore a foreign look about them, and his patchy face bore marks of a hot sun.

Sitting opposite Frank, Bodie said: 'This is the pits, Frank. Let's go up to your room.'

Frank's puffy eyelids lifted as he looked around the lounge.

'This is the Grand Ballroom. My room is the pits.'

Bodie hunched forward with that way he had of getting his coat collar up around his ears, even when it was folded down. His sleek dark head and the smoothness of him looked so out of place here he could never escape detection.

'If there's anything I can do –'

'You can.'

Bodie looked pleased. Frank Armstrong and he had fought together, in the old days, mercenaries fighting for pay, sure, but comrades in arms. He said: 'Okay.'

Frank said: 'Beat it. Don't remind me of the old days.'

Bodie winced. 'They're not so old for you, Frank. You got back here from Babwesi just last week.'

'You guys check everybody in and out the country?'

Very gently, just stating a hard fact with as much tact as possible, Bodie told Frank Armstrong: 'People like you, Frank.'

'And like *you* used to be! Now you're legal, don't make one thing wrong and the other thing right. Hell . . .' He reached his bottle and poured another slug of scotch.

Bodie took out the list of names given him by Cowley and pushed it discreetly across the table. Glass lifted, Frank squinted sideways down at the paper.

'What's this? Old home week? Giving a party? Welcome home, Frank . . .'

The list of names, to men like Bodie and Frank Armstrong, would strongly suggest a reunion.

Bodie said: 'Somebody tried to score Abraham St Jacques today.'

Frank looked astonished.

'You think *I* did?'

He held out his free hand towards Bodie. It was shaking not even a fine tremble but a real all-over shake. Try as he might, Armstrong could not conceal that shake.

'Look at me. I couldn't fire a cap pistol.' The bitterness poured out. 'Welcome home, Frank . . .'

He drank his scotch off and reached to pour another. Bodie caught the stretching arm. He forced Frank to look at the list.

'Give me the latest on any of these names.'

Frank could not break Bodie's grip. He stared blearily at the names, and then looked at Bodie.

'I'm a mercenary, pal. What's in it for me?'

Bodie was short with his old comrade.

'I won't talk about the old days.'

Frank had to laugh. It was so dire it was comic. He focused on the list. He licked his lips. He read down and shook his head as he read each name.

'None of this makes any sense. Hell, why'd anybody want to kill St Jacques?'

Bodie didn't know. If Frank didn't know where did that leave him, apart from the paddleless creek?

Doyle made his rounds, and turned up absolutely nothing. Not a single solitary lead. No one could see why they couldn't talk freely, for no one had anything to hide. It seemed to make no sense to them that Abraham St Jacques should be iced.

Doyle yawned, looked at his wristwatch, groaned, and started to plod along the street. The buildings here were in darkness at this time of night, and certain illegal card schools might offer leads. A street lamp up ahead shed a pool of light on the pavement. The smells of garbage wafted from lidless dustbins tumbled beside a wooden fence. A little wind blew bits of paper about, like puppies chasing their tails.

Shadows moved within the deeper shadows.

Into the pool of radiance from the street lamp stepped three black men, three men with mean faces, and fancy clothes, three men with their right hands dug down into their pockets.

Doyle turned to look back to where he'd parked his car.

Another black man sat on the bonnet, casually, a black blot of menace.

The leader said: 'There he is.'

Sylvester never had need to shout to make his orders understood and to have them obeyed. He led his two men towards Doyle. The four mean black faces stared at the ex-copper.

Sylvester left his men at his back and walked on alone towards Doyle. When they were close enough to see each other's faces more clearly, Sylvester smiled, and, cautiously, Doyle returned the greeting.

'I hear you're looking for me,' said Sylvester. His face was black and strong, and his teeth were white, and he carried himself well. His right hand dug into his pocket. 'You finally had enough? Decided to play it smart at last? Cut yourself in on some easy bread?'

His right hand whipped out.

The black fingers grasped an enormous roll of bills. There was money there for the good time in a big way.

Doyle said: 'When I do, you'll be the first guy I'll look up. I just want a few minutes, Sylv, and you can go back to work.'

They walked to Doyle's car and he pushed the fourth man off the bonnet. Sylvester gave a hard nod and the man joined the other two. Sylvester and Doyle got into the car.

'Man,' said Sylvester when they were alone. 'I wish I didn't owe you.'

Sylvester sounded quite different now. His toughness dropped away now he no longer, in this privacy, had to maintain his pose as the big rough tough hard topman.

'This won't cost you anything,' Doyle told him. 'Well, a few friends, maybe.'

'Friends? What's that?'

'Tell me about Abraham St Jacques.'

This shook Sylvester. This was the last thing he expected to hear about from Doyle. He spoke freely.

'We're from the same village, went to the same school. But he's in no action, he's straight, man. He's a big wheel in the diplomatic or something, you oughta know that.'

'I know that, Sylv. Thing is, he was hit today. They didn't snuff him; but they may try again. Either way, we have to find 'em.' Doyle shifted restlessly on the seat. 'Why'd it happen, Sylv? And, most important, *who* pulled the trigger, who paid him to?'

Sylvester showed his surprise. Street politics he knew about; but in the big diplomatic league – well . . . Doyle showed the list of names. Sylvester glanced at them.

'He's not important enough,' said Sylvester. 'It don't make sense. Not my scene; but I'd have had a sniff if any of the radical brothers was in on it.'

'These people may not be pros. Fanatics maybe.'

'If I knew something, that'd be different. But I don't. I'll check around, though.' He smiled, and the smile was all lop-sided. 'Always had a kind of patriotic feeling for the old country.'

Doyle nodded. 'I know. I know what you do with a lot of your ill-gotten loot.'

Sylvester looked embarrassed. Then he looked alarmed.

'Listen,' he spoke urgently, greatly concerned. 'Don't let that ever get out. If the guys thought I was into that kind of politics – hell . . . Ruin my image.'

He looked very seriously at Doyle.

'Okay,' Doyle said, taking this black man just as seriously as he was taken in his turn. 'Okay. Keep on struttin'.'

Sylvester held up the list.

'Can I keep these? I'll check 'em out for you. It's all I can do . . .'

'Okay. I'll catch you later.'

This got to Sylvester and he smiled again.

'When *you* try, and not the locals boys, then I'll think of retiring . . .'

Chortling at his own quip, he climbed out of the car.

As Doyle drove off Sylvester rejoined his cronies.

The biggest of them, a hefty fellow who could tear telephone directories in half with thumbs and little fingers, said: 'Thought he was trouble.'

'He is.' Sylvester sounded grim. Then he used that very grimness and the situation once again to emphasise his position on the street. 'All the time. But you get used to it.'

The next morning Cowley rousted his two ace operatives out early and found they had no need to be awakened. They were picked up in Cowley's car. He sat on the front passenger seat, turned to face them over the back.

The partners sat in the back. Their clothes were rumpled; but that was only the half of it.

They were unshaven, blue around the gills, their eyes were puffy and their mouths were birdcage bottom rejects from the aviary

Cowley was steamed up, his mouth pursed, his craggy face dangerous.

'Home Office, blank. MI6, blank. What about the streets?'

Doyle, wearily, said: 'Blank, too, or you'd have heard from us.'

Doubtfully, to spur his men, Cowley said: 'Your people *are* reliable?'

'They can't afford not to be.'

'What with what we let them get away with,' added Bodie. 'Look, my theory is –'

Cowley cut him off abruptly.

'You know. This *doesn't* make sense.'

Bodie and Doyle, nearer to the streets than Cowley, exchanged a look.

Cowley went on, musingly: 'Perhaps – it isn't political at all.'

'That's right.' Doyle considered. 'Something in St Jacques' private life.'

Cowley said: 'Go and find out.'

In his usual warm way, Bodie said: 'That's not *our*

department. Let the local boys handle it, if it isn't political –'

Cowley rounded on them both.

'We don't *know* it isn't. So *we're* handling it. That's the way the top brass want it, that's the way *I* want it. Get it?'

Doyle said: 'We get it.'

'So go see St Jacques. And smarten yourselves up first.'

The R/T called and Cowley answered. His craggy face expressed a little more pleasure, as though a lost traveller on a bleak mountainside had discovered half a wrecked signpost.

'They've found the gun,' he said. 'Of all places, taken down and thrown onto a bonfire on wasteland.'

Mickey Hamilton was having a nightmare – again. This nightmare was taking place in his head during the daytime – again. He lay on the sofa, twisting uncomfortably, his head rolling from side to side. He looked terrible.

And, in his head, the phantom pictures paraded and the ghastly sounds penetrated and tortured him cruelly. A woman on a delivery table, her mouth open and screaming, long and long, a long screaming agony of pain. And the surgical instruments, bright and shining, and the green gowns, dark and sombre, and the light, searing down, and the blood and the agony and the pain. Suddenly, in Mickey Hamilton's head, cutting through all that horror, the sharp sound of a slap.

The slap of a hand on bare flesh.

And then a newborn baby's first wailing cry.

Mickey Hamilton's restless writhing on the sofa as the baby cried toppled him off the edge. He fell to the floor. The thump awoke him, drove the crazy distorted memories from his mind, snapped him back to the present world, and to reality.

He blinked, licked his lips, and staggered up. He crossed to the sideboard, opened the drawer and rummaged around at the back. He pulled out a service pistol, large, bulky, ominous looking. He weighed the weapon in his hand. He nodded. A few more quick delvings into the drawer produced the silencer.

Mickey Hamilton stuck the weapon down his belt, reached over for his jacket, didn't bother to look around his flat as he went to the door. He was no longer staggering, no longer fuddled. He walked with a purpose. The task had been set to his hands, and his determination to perform that task drove the torturing images of the past from his brain.

The hospital carried on busily, attempting to ignore the horror that had taken place in the forecourt, caring for the sick. The place that Mickey Hamilton visualised as a spider waiting to suck its victims dry extended helping hands to the best of its ability to the halt and the lame. Bodie and Doyle were used to hospitals. That didn't mean they liked them any more than they had to. They went up to St Jacques.

Bandaged, groggy from sedations and operations, Abraham St Jacques tried to be of help. The partners stood, one each side of the bed, and the black and white symphony between them said: 'There's no reason. I don't understand.'

'Our people have been in touch with your people.' Bodie looked down. 'Nobody can rule out superpower intervention; but we can't trace any links here to this country.'

Doyle amplified. 'So maybe – just maybe – it's purely a personal affair. Is there anyone, any organisation, with connections here, who'd want you dead?'

St Jacques tried to smile, and winced and stopped smiling. That hurt like hell.

'You want names?'

'Names? Of course we want names.'

'Alphabetical order? You see, I'm not a very lovable man. And my countrymen are nothing if not volatile. "A". Is there an A? Ah, yes. Winston Ablutu, my wife's ex-husband . . .'

Doyle began to write down what St Jacques said. But he exchanged a weary glance with Bodie.

When they'd finished, they went out past the two armed guards at the door. They trailed off along the corridor to the lifts.

'Either the drugs they've stuffed him with have made him ramble,' said Doyle. 'Or he'd be better off dead.'

Bodie vouchsafed his opinion, with a typical Bodie curl of the lips.

'Either way – a total waste of our time.'

They left the hospital and got into their car and drove off. As they drove they passed Mickey Hamilton walking up among the crowds and for all the world looking just like anybody else visiting a sick relative. He carried no flowers, true, and he looked pretty dead beat; but he attracted no attention as he went through reception and past Out Patients and along the corridor. He went straight on through the doorway with the notice: PRIVATE. HOSPITAL STAFF ONLY.

He looked around.

On a side table a pile of white coats, used by doctors and lab technicians attracted his attention.

Mickey Hamilton donned a white coat. He fastened it and transferred the handgun from his belt to the side pocket of the white coat. He kept his right hand in that pocket.

With his fist wrapped around the butt of the gun, Mickey Hamilton went out of the room into the hospital to carry out the mission he had been called on to fulfil.

Chapter Five

He found a person who would be a part of his mission in a washroom. Two doctors were talking, technical jargon and social chit-chat all mixed together. When one of the doctors, finishing drying himself off, walked out, Mickey Hamilton entered the washroom.

The other doctor saw Hamilton approaching in the mirror above the sink.

Hamilton said: 'Pardon me. Are you a doctor?'

'Yes, of course I am. But you shouldn't –'

The man broke off in complete astonishment. His eyes opened wide and his mouth also opened, to scream. Hamilton just took the gun from his pocket, aimed it at the doctor's temple, and pulled the trigger.

The doctor was hurled against the wall and toppled sideways. His body collapsed against the sinks. Blood started to run down, mingled with the water from the tap, swirling in lurid patterns down the wastehole.

Hamilton just put the handgun back in his pocket and walked out of the door.

He walked along the corridors, passing porters pushing loaded trolleys, passing nurses and other nondescript people. No one gave him a second look. He was just a man with a white coat.

A nurse popped her head out of a door, looked across at Hamilton, and said: 'Doctor, I've got –'

Then she realised that this man in a white coat was not the doctor for whom she was looking. She had a batch of X-rays. She looked away again and spotted the man she wanted walking up after Hamilton.

'Doctor Norris. I've got the X-rays.'

As Hamilton walked on to the bend in the corridor, Doctor Norris took the X-rays from the nurse.

'Thanks, nurse. I'll take a look. Are you busy now? If these are positive I may need you right away.'

'I have to give these notes to Dr Lee. May I do that first?'

Listening from his vantage point at the bend in the corridor, Hamilton heard the doctor say: 'Yes, of course,' and then the clack of the nurse's shoes as she walked off.

Hamilton walked back around the corridor, pushed the door of the room open. Norris was pinning up the X-rays. Norris was alone.

There were no doubts in Hamilton's frazzled brain.

This was the thing he had to do. This was his divine mission. No doubts at all.

He lifted the gun, pointed it at the doctor and shot him. This was the way of it, this was the way it had to be. This was another execution for a right and just cause.

As he reached the door on his way out he swayed and clutched at the jamb to support himself.

The blood, dead men, the feel of the gun, the smell of cordite . . . No. No, he had to go on. No matter how much these executions might disgust him, this was something he must do. Had to do. He steeled himself. No matter how sick-making it was to a man of sensibility, he had to continue.

He wandered on and found himself at the entrance to one of the men's wards where a consultant, very big in his own eyes, was just completing a ward round with a flock of students in tow.

The consultant knew how to play the right tune when it came to medical students. He'd done it enough times.

'So remember, gentlemen,' he said in his grandest manner, very much the big I am among a gaggle of lesser breeds. 'Don't let them plague you with their problems. You have a job to do. Get them out, one way or another, as quickly as possible, for their own good and for the good of everyone.' He made great play with his stethoscope, using it as a conductor might use his baton. 'And never become personally involved.' He looked around, brisk, no-nonsense 'Until Thursday, then.'

As the students, suitably impressed with the old

charlatan's performance, moved off like a flock of seagulls, the doctor went into a side office.

After a moment, Mickey Hamilton went in after him.

Lily Bolsover always said she only worked as a receptionist at the hospital out of a sense of duty, that she wanted to help the sick. The greengages were not that good, either. But she met a lot of people, and the money did come in handy, on a part-time basis, when Fred was out, which was more often than not, these days.

She left her desk to help bring in an elderly lady in a wheel chair. People were milling about as usual, and the hard wooden benches were filled with the misery always to be found there when the hospital could see to them. She tucked the old lady up and helped wheel her along and then looked with amazement and indignation as young Dr Ellison – *that* young Doctor Ellison – came rushing to the desk like a maniac.

He grabbed up a phone and started punching buttons. His hair was all over his face and that face was as white as a sheet.

Lily Bolsover tut-tutted and left Albert in his white coat to get on with pushing the old lady. Lily marched back to her reception desk.

'Doctor,' she started in the tone of voice she used on young Fred Junior when he'd been up to his tricks. 'You know the rules –'

Dr Ellison just said: 'Dr Dyson's been shot –'

Lily looked shocked. Another phone rang and automatically she answered.

'Reception.'

A girl's voice on the phone, screamed: 'Help! Quickly! It's Dr Norris – he's dead and all the X-rays are –'

Lily said: 'Dead?'

Then, as the nurse on the other end of the line went on, Lily said: 'Yes, of course –' The line went dead.

She turned to Dr Ellison.

Dr Norris's dead, too.'

Receptionist and doctor stared at each other.

Then they originated the various calls they had to make and set the hospital machinery into motion.

Mickey Hamilton walked back down the rear part of the hospital, through the labyrinth of corridors, and the hospital smells went with him; disinfectant, mostly, but always there, in the background, rankling away, the raw red stink of spilled blood.

In the back area where white ambulances waited grimly and men in blue uniforms moved about, talking, smoking, waiting for the calls of life and death, Hamilton walked swiftly past. A delivery van was parked with rear doors open. Hamilton stopped in the cover of the van.

He could feel the shakes coming on him. A fine tremor through his muscles made his body twitch. He took off the white coat and then he stared at the gun in his fist.

It horrified and disgusted him.

Shaking, his face a grey mask, he wrapped the gun in the white coat and tossed it into the open back of the van.

Then he hurried unobserved through the rear gates. He moved swiftly along the pavement around to the front and caught his bus just as it was moving off.

The hospital cold room was cold.

Cowley gave a little shiver as he and Bodie and Doyle looked down on the sheet-covered bodies. They were ranked out like a display in a butcher's shop. An orderly was going around tying labels to the big toe of each left foot.

CI5 had been brought in on this one, and Cowley wanted the answers.

'And no attempt was made on St Jacques at all?'

Doyle said: 'Looks like we made one big mistake up front.'

'Yes,' said Cowley. 'Because the *killer* made one big mistake. He wasn't specifically after St Jacques at all. This wasn't political. It wasn't even personal. Our man's a psycho. He just wanted to kill.'

Bodie wrinkled his nostrils.

'This place is full of patients, porters, orderlies, nurses; but he's interested in *one* kind of victim.'

Doyle touched the tag on the nearest corpse's toe.

'Dr Dyson. Dr Norris. Dr Pagett-Munroe.'

Cowley nodded. He was persuaded.

'But what's the link? Where's the reason? Where's the sense?'

They were mystified on that one. But Doyle, his curly hair rivalling that of Medusa, was feeling philosophical enough to say: 'Well, looks like it's out of our hands now, anyway.'

'Oh, no!' snapped George Cowley. 'Oh, no. I'm not letting this go. I just took more stick from the top brass than I've done since the Borsitary foul up. We had fifteen men inside and outside the building.' He looked disgusted. 'And they were all powerless.'

A trifle warmly, Doyle said: 'There's no way CI5 can be blamed.'

'We look like mugs.' George Cowley did not like that feeling. It did not happen often, and when it did Cowley took the utmost pains to dispose of it as quickly as possible. 'So we're going to prove we are not.' He stared challengingly at the partners. 'By catching this lunatic before he gets any other clever ideas.'

'Easier said than done.' It had to be Bodie to point out the obvious.

'If it was easy,' said Cowley in his most dangerous tones, 'everybody'd be doing it and you two'd be out of a job. So jump.'

Obediently, the two ace agents of CI5 jumped.

Doyle went down to where a police quick-sketch artist was just finishing up a likeness. His slender hands worked swiftly with pencil and charcoal, rubber and whitener, over the cartridge paper. What he drew brought a frown to the nurse's face.

'Yes – I think so. I only saw him for a second. I wasn't paying attention to him. He was just an orderly.'

She glanced up at Doyle.

'Unfortunately,' said Doyle, 'he wasn't. We've checked, all staff members are accounted for. He was just somebody who came in off the streets. There are never any checks in hospital.'

'How can anyone check everyone coming in?'

'There would be ways.' Doyle shook his head. 'But for a police state.'

The nurse was still shocked by what she had witnessed.

'Maybe that's what we need with terrible things like this happening.'

'No,' Doyle told her, gently, knowing that what he said was true, even if it was apparently trite. It was one of the rocks upon which CI5 was founded. 'We have to remove the reasons for them happening, not just the opportunity.' As the nurse looked away, realising that she had been reproved if only in the gentlest way, Doyle finished: 'Well, thanks for your help. You can go.'

When all they could do had been done, the CI5 people went back to HQ for fresh developments. The handgun wrapped in a white coat had been quickly discovered and forensics had been let loose on it.

Bodie waited in the computer room as the operator fed in the numbers of the rifle and of the handgun.

'Now we'll see if there's any connection,' said the operator as her baby chungled and rumbled away to itself.

The answer printout on the screen came up.

Bodie looked pleased.

Cowley walked in, scowling, a flimsy in his hand blown backwards by the force of his entry.

'Nothing in dabs,' he said. 'Whoever he is, he's a first timer. As far as fingerprint records go.'

Bodie said: 'We've got a link between both weapons.' He nodded at the screen and the printout. 'Training Centre. Larchmount.'

'Larchmount?'

'Yeah. Looks like our bloke's an ex-soldier.'

* * *

The spring this year in the country opened up a new world for Mickey Hamilton. But he did not really notice the hedgerows bright with flowers, the lushness of the grass, the tallness of the sky and the fluffiness of the clouds. All these familiar and dear symbols of burgeoning life were lost on him as he trudged along from the coach stop towards the institution.

The letter had summoned him and, of course, he had come at once. He left the city and the hospital behind him.

Only for the moment . . .

Once the institution had been a country house, lavish amidst lavish grounds. Now the grounds were occupied by the casualties of life. The country house's function was at once explained by the notice which Hamilton passed without noticing – HOSPITAL – DRIVE CAREFULLY.

He passed up the drive to the front entrance where the Matron was waiting. On the lawns children were taking as much notice of the scenery and the birds as was Hamilton.

'Mr Hamilton,' said Matron. 'We tried to telephone but they said the line was –'

'Temporarily out of order. Didn't pay the bill.'

'Perhaps you should have done for Kathy's sake.'

Because it was true, the remark did not anger him.

'May I see her? Can I see her?'

He was led inside and to the intensive care unit. The sunshine seemed to shrivel here. He looked down into the sophisticated bubble of the oxygen tent. Kathy lay there. She was blonde and pretty, like Maureen, and she would soon be seven, and nothing mattered any more.

'I can see her,' said Hamilton. 'But she can't see me.'

'It was inevitable,' said Matron. She tried to comfort Hamilton. 'You've always known. There's nothing I can say to make it any easier, except, perhaps, when it happens, she'll just quietly slip away to where there's no pain, ever, for souls as blessed as hers.'

'She shouldn't have been this way.' Hamilton's features began to crumble.

'There's a reason, an ultimate meaning, I'm sure.'

'There *is* a reason. They didn't care, did they? Her mum was just another woman having a baby, nothing special, nothing to get worked up about so – so they didn't make the right preparations, did they? They didn't try hard enough when it started to go wrong, did they? That's the reason, isn't it? The doctors –'

'Statistically, Kathy and children like her represent a minute percentage of all births in this country.'

'Do they? That just makes me even more determined to do the right thing.'

Matron found a small smile. 'I'm sure you will.'

In his turmoil Hamilton was surprised she should agree to what he was doing. 'Really?'

'It's all you can do. Soldier on.'

Suddenly, Hamilton smiled. 'Soldier on? I will, Matron, I will. And, thanks.'

Now she was pleased for him, if a little surprised at the vehemence of his tone. He turned, looking not down at his daughter, but towards the future and the task set to his hand.

Bodie quite enjoyed his trip to Larchmount Training Centre. For one thing, he walked in on Sergeant Harry Bellager knocking seven kinds of brickdust out of a gaggle of recruits. The unarmed combat routine always impressed, and when the sergeant saw Bodie, he smiled.

'Nah then,' he boomed. 'What have we here? A new recruit? Looks like he could handle things a sight better than any three of you lot put together, don't he? Let's see how he shapes up to Dirty Henry Bellager, shall we?'

Bodie ambled forward. The recruits clustered in the gym around the mat looked apprehensive at the foolhardiness of this new wet-behind-the-ears recruit. They thought of Sergeant Bellager as Superman and the Hulk rolled into one.

The fight was fairly brief, fairly clean, and patently unfair.

Bellager had always been good. He thought he had

Bodie; then Bodie let his weight go away and Bellager wa fighting air, and going up and over to land with a soggy thump.

Bodie stretched down a hand.

'Should have told you up front, Harry. I'm in CI5 now.'

Bellager's looks spoke volumes of expletives, and then Captain Tepper wandered in with the files Bodie had asked for and it was back to On Parade again. Still, it had reminded Bodie, the ex-para, of old army days.

They soon established that weapons and explosives had gone missing, not many and infrequently, but some. It was all a matter of difficulty and record-keeping.

'Every man on the base was cleared of suspicion at the time,' said Captain Tepper. He wore a Sam Browne, which made him look conspicuous. 'Someone who knew the camp and could sneak in. There was no way we could follow up on every man who'd served here.'

'Well, maybe we can. Give me a list of everyone who served here, left the service or was transferred in, say, six months before the thefts were discovered.'

'That's a helluvan administrative request.'

'It's a helluva needle in a helluva haystack too, Captain.'

Ray Doyle got to ask the computer the questions; rather he brought the stack of files in for the computer operator to rattle out the questions. She groaned at the size of the stack.

'Time to feed baby,' said Doyle.

'Looks like the day-to-day reporting of the Hundred Years War.'

'You're ninety years out. But it's a war all right. This is everybody who died in that hospital in the last ten years.'

Cowley walked in, with his usual knack of being on the spot, and asked: 'Will you have this fed by the time Bodie's back?'

The operator, gloomily, said: 'If he's coming on foot.'

'A link between a hospital patient and a soldier at Larchmount,' said Cowley, unmoved. 'Ask it what the odds are.'

When the question was fed in, the computer simply screened: COMPUTATION IMPOSSIBLE BASED ON KNOWN DATA INPUT.

'In other words,' said Doyle, 'lousy.'

'But you could be right. Why else would he go back to the hospital again if the building itself, something that happened there, isn't the reason?'

'He's probably got a death wish.'

'I noticed.' Cowley took off his glasses. 'He wishes some doctors dead and makes his wish come true.'

'I mean, going back there, it's as if the enormity of the thing is making him look for a comparable punishment. He's looking to be caught. He wanted to do it; but at the same time he didn't. It's like a cry for help. It's a classic text book syndrome, it's –'

'Okay, okay. A little less Freud, a lot more action.'

'Sure,' said Doyle. 'But I think we have another problem. But – no, you don't want to know. It's just more Freud.'

'Like what?'

'Well, if I've figured this out right, like what's he going to do next?'

'You're right,' Cowley said. 'I don't want to know.'

He was worried. Of course he wanted to know what this maniac would do next, he'd just responded to Doyle's words. But, the big question was, what?

Having a mission in life and wanting to carry it out were very different from actually standing up and doing it.

Hamilton could remember with vivid horror the blood and the way that doctor's brains had blown out. He tried to shut these awful images from his mind. He needed more assurance, even, than Matron had given him.

When he walked into the church he was dwarfed by the size of the structure. Pillars lifted, perpendicular, soaring, lofting, fanning out into intricate patterns, superbly beautiful. Stained glass muted and mellowed the light, made of it a glorious chiaroscuro. The sounds of life were both diminished and enhanced in the church. Echoes fell like the brushing of doves' wings, vaulting and rolling away into dusty corners.

He bumped into a portly priest in the porch as he turned, giving up the idea of finding any hope here.

'It's Mickey Hamilton, Father. You remember?'

The priest sort of did and didn't remember; but he was a man who believed in trying.

'Yes, yes, of course. I'm glad you're here – after so long.'

'Father – The Lord giveth and the Lord taketh away.'

'Yes, yes.'

'Vengeance is mine, sayeth the Lord.' Hamilton's tones caused the priest concern. 'It's not what we do, it's why we do it. Is it a sin to try to save life? To prevent suffering?'

'No of course not.'

'Even if in the process people suffer, too?'

The priest grasped for the appropriate phrase.

'Sometimes we have to be cruel to be kind. Remember, too, we can also kill with kindness.'

Hamilton said, on a breath: 'Is that a sin, to kill with kindness?'

The priest smiled to himself in satisfaction in being able to take refuge in casuistry. 'Is a figure of speech a sin? I can hardly say it is without knowing more.'

'It isn't a sin?'

'The Lord said Thou shalt not kill. But killing with kindness may be different.'

'Will you bless me, then?'

'Are your motives pure?'

'Yes, Father. For the sake of other children. For the sake of their mothers. Will you bless me?'

The priest could not really make head or tail of this; but the earnestness of this man impressed him. He glanced at his watch, saw he was late, and decided to humour Mickey Hamilton.

'For the sake of other children and their mothers? Yes, you have my blessing.'

'Thank you, Father.'

Hamilton walked off. He went with a firm step and his head was up. The priest turned away to hurry off to his meeting when abruptly he recalled Mickey Hamilton.

He swung back and called out.

'Mickey Hamilton! Of course. I conducted the service for your wife's funeral, didn't I?'

But Hamilton was hurrying out and away from the church. The priest followed to the door, and called again. 'Wait – Mr Hamilton!'

But Mickey Hamilton was gone about the Lord's business.

The burden on Mickey Hamilton remained; but it was lightened. He felt refreshed. He still looked a sloppy mess; but that had not worried him since Maureen died.

He went into a newsagent to buy an evening paper, and then wandered along to the pub and stood outside, waiting for it to open. He scanned the paper casually.

His attention was caught by a photograph of an African gentleman in full tribal regalia.

He glanced at this and then saw the headlines just beneath, detailing the arrival of various worthies at Heathrow, and leading off with a good catchline: 'Witch Doctor at Conference.' This was just a gimmicky newspaper story; but he read the rest of the story carefully.

He did not go into the pub. He tucked the paper under his arm and caught the bus home.

In his flat he went straight to the cupboard and, kneeling down, rummaged about inside.

He brought out bundles of plastic explosives, fuses, wire. His face was absorbed, concentrated, as he set to work. His face was the face of a dedicated man at his devotions.

Chapter Six

The sprawling complex of the conference centre lazed under the spring sunshine like a lazy beast on the wide savannah in prehistoric times. Flags fluttered from ranked staffs. People moved purposefully about and Hamilton had no difficulty walking in.

Notice boards proclaimed 7th INTERNATIONAL MEDICAL CONGRESS.

Hamilton walked in through the main doors carrying his plastic shopping bag from the supermarket.

Workmen were putting finishing touches to the interior decorations, electricians were wiring up the speakers and lighting, and girls were unwrapping parcels of leaflets and programmes at the tables in the main entrance lobby. It was easy enough for Hamilton to pick up a programme and agenda and then walk on into the echoing expanses of the building's interior.

He went up the stairs into the balcony. The shadows fell here with a thick warm comfort about his shoulders. His face, grey and worn, was now composed. He knew what he was going to do. He would have to be precise. He looked down from the balcony onto the spreading expanse of seating, looked under the pillars along the sides, checked the main doors. Yes, that would do nicely. Thoughtfully, he began to take his little plastic packages out of the plastic shopping bag.

The computer room in CI5 HQ was generally a busy place and today it fairly hummed with activity. The computer had been fed what amounted to the statistics of the Hundred Years War – more or less – and now the operator turned in the seat.

'Here's the connection,' she called.

Cowley, Bodie and Doyle hastened across.

The computer screen flashed out what had taken so much trouble and application to discover. A single name shone up.

MICHAEL ARTHUR HAMILTON.

Cowley said: 'Get the address. We'll try to pick him up.'

When their car reached the drab wasteland that was the address the records carried for Hamilton the three CI5 men stared out in fury.

'Urban renewal,' said Cowley. 'Have to find out where he's rehoused.'

The Rover three and a half started up, and Doyle dropped off at the hospital to pursue that end of the enquiry. He found the right doctor at last and a few moments' conversation gave Doyle a little inkling of the complexity of the situation. He didn't say, as he might very well have done: 'Look, doc, there's a nutter running about shooting quacks.' Instead, he said: 'I'm not talking about records. This is human beings we're dealing with. What about memories?'

The doctor flushed just a trifle. 'Look, the baby was born what –'

'Seven years ago. Here in this hospital.'

'The mother died four years ago.'

'Here in this hospital?'

'It's a long time. That's my point.'

'Not for him. Other people died here in this hospital. Yesterday.'

'You think he did it? Because of what happened to his family?' The shock caught the doctor by the throat.

'Looks that way,' said Doyle. 'And he may well be planning something else.'

'Perhaps one of the staff can help – Sister Noel.'

Doyle caught up with Sister Noel over in the corner of Reception. She it was who had found Doctor Pagett-Munroe with his head blown off. She was still shocked. Doyle handled her carefully, not wishing to upset her even more.

'Four years ago a woman was admitted after taking a massive dose of sleeping pills. Maureen Hamilton. You attended her, Sister.'

'I was a nurse then. I can't remember every patient –'

'Checking the records . . . It was a busy night. She was admitted at 1.05, and treatment didn't start until 1.45.'

She brushed her hand across her forehead under the starched cap. She was quite clearly a good woman in the best sense of that phrase; but she was also human. 'You've no idea of the hours we put in. You can't treat people properly when you've been under pressure for ten, sometimes eleven, hours.'

'I understand the problems. I'm just trying to get information about the husband, Michael Hamilton.'

Sister Noel nodded, remembering because: 'He must have been the one who became violent. Had to be sedated. Said he should never have brought her here; but it's the only hospital in seven miles.' She drew a breath. 'Yes, I remember. He claimed she would have lived if she'd been treated in time.'

Doyle had to ask. He didn't like it, but he had to know.

'Would she?'

'Frankly – I don't know. It was a massive overdose. But –'

'Their baby was born here, too. And that went badly. The child had Oxymoph –'

Sister Noel nodded numbly, the implications already apparent to her. 'Oxymophileia. That would cause terrible brain damage. Oh, the poor man.'

'Now he's on a killing spree.'

'Have you talked to his sister? She handled the arrangements after the death. He'd broken down. I think he had to go into an institution.'

'That's not in the records.'

'It wouldn't be. That's just the patient's history. You need to look into the necrology, what happens after they die.'

'Then I should do that right away. Thank you, Sister.'

When Doyle reported in the latest development, Cowley told him to go right round to the sister's and check it out. The R/T crackled as Cowley went on filling out the picture.

'We've scored, too. Hamilton's new address, traced through the local council. We're on our way.'

When Cowley reached the block of flats where Hamilton lived he saw Bodie sitting on a wall swinging his legs.

Cowley said: 'I think I'd go mad if I had to live here. He's on the top floor.'

They walked shoulder to shoulder across the cracked concrete, past the alcoves containing dustbins and other areas with washing lines and no washing – anything hung up there was likely to disappear, so it was said – and went into the entrance.

Cowley peered at the lift, finger raised to press the button. The sign said OUT OF ORDER. That sign showed a lot of use.

They looked disgusted and started climbing the stairs when Doyle raced into the lobby, like them starting for the lift and then hurrying up the stairs. Cowley and Bodie stopped.

'Why aren't you going to the sister's?' demanded Cowley.

'This is the address,' Doyle told him. 'Hamilton lives here too?'

Laconically, with a heavenward roll of his expressive eyes, Bodie said: 'Penthouse suite.'

Cowley, impatient, said: 'Let's tell it climbing.'

Whilst Doyle talked to Kay Costa, Cowley and Bodie trudged on up higher towards Hamilton's flat.

Kay was quite clearly concerned for her brother, and demanded to know what he had done. Her manner convinced Doyle that she had been expecting something to happen. He knew damn well she had no idea that it would be what it was.

He made her sit down. 'You've been expecting him to do something bad, have you?'

'Well, he's been, you know, a bit funny since he came out

of the institution. Of course, he never was himself after Maureen's death. What's he done? Please tell me.'

Doyle held up the newspaper which contained the story. 'There's no easy way to tell you. We think he did this.'

Kay saw the headlines, and the horror hit her, and she put her hand to her mouth. Doyle thought she was going to be sick. He saw she was on the point of breaking up, and knew he had to move quickly before she did, for the sake of whoever it was her brother was going to kill next – whatever doctor it was that her brother was going to kill next.

He got through to her, for a moment, and talked her into finding the photographs he needed. She was weeping now, not crying or sobbing or shrieking; but weeping.

'Here he is with Maureen – and here they are with Kathy.'

'And the address of the home in case we need to know?'

'Yes – I'll get it for you. It's near Reading.' Her voice trembled as she wept. 'There they are when they got married.'

The photograph in this context was dramatically pathetic. What had white wedding gowns, and bouquets of flowers and lace and bridesmaids to do with blood and murder? Perhaps a damn sight more than people were prepared to admit . . . The white gown was the clue, of course, and the type of blood, and the flowers smelling this springtime . . .

Cowley panted up the stairs as Bodie leaped up four at a time. That damn bullet the Condor Legion had put in his leg in Spain must be shifting around an awful lot. Anyway, he couldn't make it like Bodie.

'For once,' he said in his tough voice. 'You can go in without me.'

Bodie called down: 'If you're not up in ten minutes I'll send for a St Bernard.'

All the same, Bodie used the technique to break into Hamilton's flat, and he drew his handgun before he went in. Anyway, the flat was empty. He was giving it a preliminary search when Cowley appeared at the open door. Cowley crunched over the broken glass where Bodie had made his entry, and then as he rounded the corner he and Bodie came face to face.

Each man had a gun pointed at the other.

Bodie said: 'Nobody home.'

Cowley lowered his automatic. He panted. The climb up all those damn stairs had thwacked him sideways.

'How – how many . . .'

He panted for breath, so to help him out, Bodie said: 'How many rooms?'

'How – how many flights of stairs was that?'

He staggered into the lounge and flopped down onto the sofa. He was breathing hard. He looked around at the mess.

'If his mind is anything like the state of this place . . .'

With the nose of a professional Bodie sniffed out the hiding place where Hamilton stashed his arsenal. He came up with a couple of revolvers and some handgrenades from the cupboard.

The sound of footfalls from outside, crunching over the broken glass, brought both men up ready with handguns drawn.

It was Ray Doyle.

He rolled in and flopped down beside Cowley.

He started to tell his news, saying: 'Least we know – phew –' and broke off for a breath.

Cowley, just about recovered from the climb now, looked very severely at the ex-copper.

'When did you last take the CI5 physical?'

' – what he looks like,' finished Doyle as he got his breath and grandly ignored the chief's unkind query.

Bodie broke in to say: 'There should be explosives here, according to the army.'

Cowley looked at the photograph Doyle handed across. Cowley put his glasses on with that typical sideways jerk of the head. His lips pursed up. He took his glasses off and said: 'Maybe you were right.'

Bodie, being Bodie, said: 'Of course.' Then, carefully; 'But about what in particular?'

Cowley said: 'About "What's he going to do next?" If the stuff's not hidden somewhere else, he's running loose with enough explosives to cause a very big hole in some part of London.'

Doyle said: 'I got the address of the place where they take care of the kiddy. Maybe he's gone there.'

'Well, check it out then for God's sake!'

Doyle scowled, half for the implied rebuke, half for the way in which it revealed that George Cowley, Chief of CI5, was becoming frazzled over this case.

As Doyle moved to pick up the telephone he pushed the newspaper aside – the newspaper Hamilton had been reading.

Cowley suddenly leaned forward.

The newspaper was opened and folded, and Cowley saw the picture of an African dressed in tribal gear. He read.

Then he looked up at his two top agents.

'I know it's a silly question. But – what do you get at a medical congress?'

'Doctors. Lots of doctors.'

Doyle put the phone down. Bodie started for the door. Cowley levered himself up. Bullet or no damn bullet in the leg, he had to make it down those stairs. Now if he was a secret agent or super-sophisticated spy with a great deal of money and facilities galore at his finger tips he'd just call out for a chopper to pick him off the roof . . .

He could call out on the R/T for the uniformed local branch to go in and supervise the preliminary moves. By the time they reached the conference centre Cowley, Bodie and Doyle entered a scene of orderly confusion. The police were escorting the delegates out only moments after they had begun to gather together. Plainclothes police marksmen were entering the building by side and rear entrances. Some plastic explosive charges had already been discovered hidden under carpets by the seating. It was clear that Hamilton had mingled with the workmen busy over the last minute details and laid his charges with little trouble.

Bodie and Doyle eased into the deserted auditorium.

They flicked their gazes about in a quick survey of the area. Rows of seats, that was the first impression, and batteries of lights, and tall drapes, and the balcony.

'This might be the place,' said Bodie, quietly. He climbed up to the gallery as Doyle walked slowly towards the front looking for more plastic charges.

As Bodie climbed up and then edged along the first row of gallery seating on the balcony, Mickey Hamilton, hiding in the shadows, saw him.

Hamilton's shock was reflected openly on his face. He reached toward the plastic bag for his revolver, and knocked it against the metal support between two seats. The gun gonged.

Bodie ducked down instantly.

He hauled out his R/T and spoke in a hushed voice into the mouthpiece.

'I think he's up here . . .'

Doyle's response came at once.

'Has he seen you?'

'Must have done.'

'Then get out of there!'

Bodie waited, and then said 'Can't very well, without being sure.'

He left the handset of the R/T on and, suddenly, in a good firm voice called out.

'Mr Hamilton? We know it's you. We know what you've done. We know why you did it.'

The voice coming from some hidden space between the seating disturbed Mickey Hamilton. His face still showed shock. They knew? He thought about things for a moment, a jumbled crazy train of thought that had only one logical end, and that was what brought him to his feet, out in full view.

In his left hand he held the revolver. In his right the small detonating device that would trigger the charges he had planted, planted with cunning knowledge, did not tremble.

Bodie stood up, too, watching cautiously.

Mickey Hamilton half-smiled. It was a ghastly parody of a human emotion.

'Do you know what I'm going to do? I'm going to press this detonator and this hall explodes, you and me and the doctors with it.'

Over the open channel of the R/T both Cowley and Doyle listened in. Cowley gave urgent orders to the police. Doyle continued to look for the explosives. He had fathomed out the plan, crazy as it was, and the pattern in which Hamilton had planted his charges.

Doyle took out his knife and went into the business of wire cutting.

Up above him Bodie faced Hamilton.

'There aren't going to be any doctors,' Bodie told the crazed man – if truly crazed he was in this context – and watched for the first hint of a normal reaction. 'It'll be just us, and that's a waste of good explosives.'

Mickey Hamilton smiled beatifically.

He was no longer fully there, not really, not really taking it all in, hell-bent on his divine mission.

'Killing with kindness. I've been absolved.'

Bodie looked worried that he wasn't getting through to this man. The explosives worried him, too, of course; but they had to come after convincing this man not to press the button that would blow them all to hell past breakfast time.

'We've come to know a lot about you, Mickey. I was talking to Kay just a while back. Showed me some snaps of you and Maureen and Kathy. I've got a couple here.'

That had been a chance. But – 'Don't talk about them.'

His thumb hovered over the detonating device's button.

Cutting another fuse from the pile of plastic explosive like a humped heap of unmentionables under the next seat, Doyle sweated blood searching out the other humps and their fuses.

'How many to go?' demanded Cowley on the R/T.

'Two – maybe three.'

The police super in charge had his marksmen ready now, on the line, waiting to get a bead on the maniac. They were tooled up, ready to go, waiting their opportunity.

Micky Hamilton went on talking to Bodie.

'I'm not doing this for revenge. I'm thinking of the future. The pain and suffering I'm going to save.'

'No you're not.' Bodie risked being a little tougher of tone. 'You think they killed your wife. She killed herself.'

Hamilton shook his head in the tides of misery that swamped up and over his resolve.

'They could have saved her.'

'She took an overdose.'

'She blamed herself for Kathy! But that was their fault, too. Now she's dying. Kathy's dying. She's seven, only seven, why should they get away with it?'

Bodie sweated out the answer as Doyle, down below on the floor among the seating called into his handset.

'Last one.'

Cowley's voice was firm. He had to be firm. If the job was distasteful, then the heat of the kitchen would be too much for the chief of CI5. He gave his orders.

'Fire when ready.'

Bodie heard. The news from Doyle lifted his immediate concern; but he wanted to talk to Hamilton. Bodie liked to put on the rough tough hard façade. And, by God, he was tough! But Bodie was human, almost just like anyone else. He had seen enough suffering and pain, too damn much. He had no desire to cause any more to people who had passed beyond their limit of tolerance, unless he believed it necessary.

For Mickey Hamilton Bodie, who had heard all the story, could feel only sorrow and remorse that society could act in the way that society could act.

'Mickey –' he began.

But his feelings about Hamilton were accurate. The man was past normal feelings, past remorse, past caring. He wanted to go.

He pressed the detonator button.

He looked up, shocked out of his stupor that gave him strength to do just the one thing, and found he had strength for another . . .

He lifted the revolver, aimed it –

The police marksmen fired.

Their shots crashed out.

A window pane burst in a spinning shower of fragments.

A fusillade of bullets hit Mickey Hamilton.

He catapulted over, toppling and sliding helplessly down to the bottom of the gallery. The revolver spun away.

Bodie jumped down and knelt beside Hamilton.

They looked at each other.

Bodie was not sure if Hamilton spoke to take his mind off the pain or through the pain, or if he was in pain at all A man hit like that often felt nothing, just lay back and died.

Hamilton did not sound bitter or angry or resigned. He just sounded curious.

'How'd you know – about the – the overdose and – and everything?'

'It's the job.'

Lame, Bodie said to himself ferociously, lame. But true

Doyle was hurrying up, concerned.

Hamilton's head lolled.

'Oh.' He sounded as though he was pleased to know. 'How'd you know I'd be here?'

Doyle, kneeling on the other side of the dying man, said. 'We saw the paper in your flat.'

Now Hamilton was resigned to their omnipotence. The shadows closed in on him from all sides. But he could still speak.

'So you saw Kathy too, then?'

'Your little girl? No, we didn't see Kathy.'

'She couldn't have told you anything I suppose. That's why you didn't see her.'

Bodie said: 'S'pose so.'

Draggingly, getting his breath, and, now, painfully,

Hamilton said: 'She's what this was all about. You ought to have seen her. Go and see her.' His head rolled. 'If she's – you know . . Go and see her. Maybe you'll see why I thought – I mean . . . I really thought – they shouldn't get away with it . . .'

And, in his brain those dreadful sounds superimposed themselves on everything else. The sounds of his wife in pain, and the panicky calls for oxygen, oxygen, oxygen . . .

Bodie and Doyle stood up and away to the side as the ambulancemen carried Hamilton off. He looked forlorn on the stretcher.

Cowley joined them.

He said: 'He'll probably live . . .'

No one could be sure. Hospitals these days could perform miracles of healing, even on bodies ripped by rifle fire.

'If,' said Bodie, 'you call it living.'

Cowley would not temporise.

'It had to be done.'

Doyle said: 'Somebody should have helped him long before all this.'

'Maybe nobody could have.' Bodie remembered the way Hamilton had looked and sounded, with the detonating device in his hand.

'I don't believe that!'

'Neither do I, Bodie,' said Cowley.

Bodie turned away.

'Why do you always have to be right?'

The three watched sombrely as the ambulancemen carried the stretcher away.

For Hamilton, this had been his big day, the time when he faced anger and death in pursuit of what he thought to be the right thing. For the men of CI5, that was what they did as part of the job.

Any time. Any day.

DEEP BENEATH THE SEA
A DEADLY TRAP AWAITS . . .

SEA LEOPARD

Craig Thomas

The British nuclear submarine *HMS Proteus* carries the most sophisticated anti-detection equipment in the world. Codenamed 'LEOPARD', the top-secret anti-sonar systems render *Proteus* undetectable to the Russians. Sea trials completed, *Proteus*' first mission is to chart the new Soviet underwater defence system which poses the most deadly threat to NATO's northern flank.

But *Proteus* picks up a distress signal. From a Soviet submarine lying crippled on the sea floor. And as she sets out on her rescue mission the Russians prepare to spring a devastating deathtrap twenty fathoms beneath the ocean . . .

ADVENTURE/THRILLER 0 7221 8453 0 £1.95

I, SAID THE SPY

by Derek Lambert

Fact: Each year a nucleus of the wealthiest and most influential members of the Western world meet to discuss the future of the world's superpowers at a secret conference called Bilderberg.

A glamorous millionairess just sighting loneliness from the foothills of middle-age . . . a French industrialist whose wealth matches his masochism and meanness . . . a whizz-kid of the seventies conducting a life-long love affair with diamonds, these are just three of the Bilderbergers who have grown to confuse position with invulnerability. A mistake which could prove lethal when a crazed assassin is on the loose . . . a journalist dedicated to exposing the conference infiltrates their midst . . . and intelligence agents from Moscow, Washington and London penetrate Bilderberg's defences to reveal a conspiracy of mind-boggling proportions . . .

I, SAID THE SPY is a novel on a grand scale which sweeps the reader along on a wave of all-out excitement and suspense until the final stunning climax.

ADVENTURE/THRILLER **0 7221 5346 5** **£1.75**